Despite the cold cream on her face and the towel on her head, something about CJ Maxey demanded respect.

Her quiet dignity gave Clint pause.

Clint was no monk, not by a long shot. He'd had his share of flings, but that's all they'd been— brief romps with women no more interested in attachments than he.

But this was different. CJ was a wild card, her true nature completely unknown to him.

Warning bells clanged, and stoplights flashed.

The smart thing to do? Rein in his appetite. Put a lid on his libido. Get the story on this delectable Dairy Princess. And get out of town!

Dear Reader,

Our resolution is to start the year with a bang in Silhouette Special Edition! And so we are featuring Peggy Webb's *The Accidental Princess*—our pick for this month's READERS' RING title. You'll want to use the riches in this romance to facilitate discussions with your friends and family! In this lively tale, a plain Jane agrees to be the local Dairy Princess and wins the heart of the bad-boy reporter who wants her story…among other things.

Next up, Sherryl Woods thrills her readers once again with the newest installment of THE DEVANEYS—*Michael's Discovery.* Follow this ex-navy SEAL hero as he struggles to heal from battle—and save himself from falling hard for his beautiful physical therapist! Pamela Toth's *Man Behind the Badge,* the third book in her popular WINCHESTER BRIDES miniseries, brings us another stunning hero in the form of a flirtatious sheriff, whose wild ways are numbered when he meets—and wants to rescue—a sweet, yet reclusive woman with a secret past. Talking about secrets, a doctor hero is stunned when he finds a baby— maybe even *his* baby—on the doorstep in Victoria Pade's *Maybe My Baby,* the second book in her BABY TIMES THREE miniseries. Add a feisty heroine to the mix, and you have an instant family.

Teresa Southwick delivers an unforgettable story in *Midnight, Moonlight & Miracles.* In it, a nurse feels a strong attraction to her handsome patient, yet she doesn't want him to discover the *real* connection between them. And Patricia Kay's *Annie and the Confirmed Bachelor* explores the blossoming love between a self-made millionaire and a woman who can't remember her past. Can their romance survive?

This month's lineup is packed with intrigue, passion, complex heroines and heroes who never give up. Keep your own resolution to live life romantically, with a treat from Silhouette Special Edition. Happy New Year, and happy reading!

Karen Taylor Richman
Senior Editor

Please address questions and book requests to:
Silhouette Reader Service
U.S.: 3010 Walden Ave., P.O. Box 1325, Buffalo, NY 14269
Canadian: P.O. Box 609, Fort Erie, Ont. L2A 5X3

The Accidental Princess

PEGGY WEBB

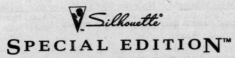

SPECIAL EDITION™

Published by Silhouette Books

America's Publisher of Contemporary Romance

For my enchanting new grandson,
William, with love

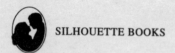 SILHOUETTE BOOKS

ISBN 0-373-24516-5

THE ACCIDENTAL PRINCESS

Copyright © 2003 by Peggy Webb

This edition published by arrangement with Harlequin Books S.A.

Visit Silhouette at www.eHarlequin.com

Printed in U.S.A.

Books by Peggy Webb

Silhouette Special Edition

Summer Hawk #1300
Warrior's Embrace #1323
Gray Wolf's Woman #1347
Standing Bear's Surrender #1384
Invitation to a Wedding #1402
*The Smile of an Angel #1436
*Bittersweet Passion #1449
*Force of Nature #1461
The Accidental Princess #1516

Silhouette Intimate Moments

13 Royal Street #447

Silhouette Romance

When Joanna Smiles #645
A Gift for Tenderness #681
Harvey's Missing #712
Venus DeMolly #735
Tiger Lady #785
Beloved Stranger #824
Angel at Large #867

*The Westmoreland Diaries

PEGGY WEBB

and her two chocolate Labs live in a hundred-year-old house not far from the farm where she grew up. "A farm is a wonderful place for dreaming," she says. "I used to sit in the hayloft and dream of being a writer." Now, with two grown children and more than forty-five romance novels to her credit, the former English teacher confesses she's still a hopeless romantic and loves to create the happy endings her readers love so well.

When she isn't writing, she can be found at her piano playing blues and jazz, or in one of her gardens planting flowers. A believer in the idea that a person should never stand still, Peggy recently taught herself carpentry.

Dear Reader,

I'm thrilled to be part of Silhouette's innovative READERS' RING. Finally the rest of the world will see what authors, editors and loyal fans of the romance genre have known all along: these wonderful love stories with the happy endings are as complex and well crafted as any books on the market. Do romance novels have tightly woven plots and well-defined themes? You bet. Do they have lovable but multifaceted characters who grow and change in the course of the story? Absolutely. Are they rich with sense of place, symbolism and lyrical language? Yes, indeed.

You have long appreciated the wonder of romance novels. I'm delighted that you can now use the questions at the back as a guide to discuss these books, perhaps discover new ways of looking at them and even get an inkling of what goes on in the minds of the authors who write them.

So gather a circle of friends, grab a cup of coffee (or perhaps a mint julep!) and spend a lovely afternoon with CJ Maxey, Clint Garrett and a host of zany Southern characters who populate Hot Coffee, Mississippi.

Happy reading!

Peggy Webb

Chapter One

Leaning back so the chair tilted dangerously on two legs Blake Dix asked, "You know any pretty women in this one-horse town I can date?"

C.J. started to say she was the church's secretary, not a matchmaking service, but she decided to bridle her tongue. After all, Blake Dix, the new music director at Trinity Baptist Church, had recently arrived in Hot Coffee, Mississippi, from Las Vegas. He was probably in culture shock.

"You might try hanging out at Chat 'N Chew BarBQ. That's the only spot in Hot Coffee that has any action."

"Thanks for the tip." The chair banged against the worn wooden floor as Blake stood up and tossed a bundle of papers on her desk. "Would you type those for me? I need them by tomorrow."

"Sure. I'll rearrange my social calendar."

"You're a hoot, C.J."

She wanted to throw her shoe at him and yell, "I could have a social life if I wanted to," which was a baldfaced lie.

It's true that she lacked grace and beauty, but women homelier than she had lovers and husbands and babies and sweet little houses all their own. C.J. didn't know what she was doing wrong. Maybe her expectations were too high. Maybe she should settle for less than intelligence and integrity and kindness. And it wouldn't hurt if they were good-looking, to boot. Maybe she should quit longing for excess and be satisfied with the likes of Leonard Lumpkin who wanted to move her to his farm and make her a domestic goddess.

Maybe she should just quit dreaming.

She did, temporarily. C.J. set to work typing. If she hurried she would be home by eight o'clock. Not that it mattered. Nobody was waiting for her except her dad, and he would barely notice what time she got home. Just the same, she stopped typing long enough to call and say she'd be late.

She was the only twenty-five-year-old she knew still living with her daddy. Not that she minded taking care of Sam: in addition to being a wonderful parent, he was the only hero she'd ever had.

In high school everybody had said C.J. was "going places." So far the only place she'd gone was to Itawamba Junior College only fifty miles from home.

Not that she minded home, either. C.J. liked the little yellow cottage on the outskirts of town. She enjoyed the pecan trees in the front yard and the big pasture in back that harbored an assortment of strays her father had collected over the years—a Siamese cat, four dogs of undetermined lineage and Suzy the fat cow. The animals were the only evidence left that Sam had once been the county's finest veterinarian. C.J. had planned to follow in his footsteps, perhaps even set up practice with him, but *the accident* changed everything.

She pushed the accident from her mind as she drove home. When she turned into the familiar driveway she saw Ellie Jones's little red VW bug parked in front of the house. It wasn't unusual to see Ellie there. She and C.J.'s mother, Phoebe, had been best friends as well as sorority sisters. Since Phoebe's death Ellie had been a mother to C.J., a quiet strong presence hovering over her and Sam like a guardian angel.

C.J. found Ellie and Sam on the back porch drinking lemon balm tea, he still in bedroom slippers and she in tennis shoes with her feet propped up on the railing.

"Ellie! You look wonderful."

"Piffle. I'm a dried-up old prune with a face like the map of China. Sit. I brought cookies."

"Macadamia nut?"

"What else?"

"Yum." C.J. grabbed three, nevermind the calories. The only thing she had in her favor was the fact that no matter how much she ate she was still so skinny she could stand sideways and you'd never know she was there.

"I came to see if you'd be Lee County's Dairy

Princess,'' Ellie said, and C.J. nearly choked on her cookie.

"This is a joke, right?"

"No. I won't beat around the bush, C.J."

"Have you ever?" Sam said, deadpan.

"Nobody entered the local pageant and I need a contestant to represent Lee County in the state's pageant. There's scholarship money, not much on the local level, but it will be yours automatically when you assume the title. The state's scholarship is big enough to put you through vet school."

"I think you should do it, C.J.," Sam said.

C.J. figured her chance of winning the state's scholarship money was as remote as her chance of turning into a raving beauty overnight, but that didn't mean she wasn't willing to help an old friend. As the county's Extension Agent, Ellie was responsible for the local Dairy Princess pageant as well as overseeing the 4-H Clubs and homemaking activities for the entire county. In view of all Ellie had done for them over the last six years, being princess by default was the least C.J. could do.

"Would I have to parade onstage in a swimsuit?"

"No. Evening gown only. That, plus give a speech about the dairy industry."

The only time C.J. ever gave a speech, she broke out in hives. This Dairy Princess business was sounding worse by the minute. Still, she owed Ellie and certainly didn't want to hurt her feelings. Maybe she could find a graceful way out.

"I don't know anything about the dairy industry. I probably don't even qualify. What about Sandi Wentworth? She's a natural," C.J. added.

Sandi had grown up next door with only her grandmother to guide her. She was more than a friend to C.J. She was like a sister.

"She doesn't qualify. Too old and no dairy herd."

"That leaves me out. I don't have a dairy herd."

"Yes, you do."

"Suzy?"

"A herd of one. Fatten her up and she'll pass for two."

"That takes care of the cow, but what about me? There's only so much a push-up bra and a new hairstyle can do."

"I'll help," Ellie said, and that's when C.J. knew she was in trouble. Ellie's only brush with beauty was the roses she grew, and as far as glamour went, nobody had seen her legs since 1979. Ellie Jones wore khakis everywhere. She added a black jacket for somber occasions and red for festive.

Still…C.J.'s mother had been considered the most beautiful woman in Lee County, if not the whole state of Mississippi, and had collected beauty queen trophies the way other girls collected charms for their bracelets. C.J. had always had a secret yen to be like her mother.

"I'll do it," she said.

"You want me to what?"

"Cover the local Dairy Princess."

The irony didn't escape Clint Garrett. He'd covered a beauty queen or two in his time, but not in the way the editor of the *Hot Coffee Tribune* meant.

"I'm a crime reporter, Wayne," he said, which was mostly true. The last big crime in Hot Coffee was when Eldridge Messingame stole Luther Arkett's Brahmin bull. Except for an occasional break-in and a purse-snatching incident every now and then, Hot Coffee didn't have any crime. Clint's job was cushy. Most days he could ride around on his motorcycle listening to country-western songs.

He covered funerals and society events to fill in the gap. Actually, the biggest society event in Hot Coffee *was* a funeral, which suited Clint just fine. He wasn't looking for fame and fortune; he was looking for a way to drift through life with the least amount of effort and attachment.

The only woman he'd ever cared about had died—his mother. When he'd come home from school crying because the other kids called him "bastard," she'd say, "That's all right, son. Just hold your head up. Someday you'll really be somebody."

She'd died while he was still in college, and took the heart right out of his dreams. Without the anchor of her love, he had become a drifter. His current lifestyle required nothing of him except to exist on the most elemental level—eat, drink and sleep, with an occasional fling thrown in.

"You *could* be a crime reporter, Clint, and a damned good one." From time to time Wayne tried to play father to Clint and make him see the error of his ways. It never worked, though. Clint knew how to dodge good intentions. "What beats me is why you bury your talent in a little burg like Hot Coffee."

"Maybe I'm like you, Wayne."

Wayne turned red all the way to the top of his bald head, then cleared his throat. "Difference between me and you is that you're half my age. I wasted my life.

I hate to see you waste yours. You're the best reporter I've got.''

"I'm the only one you've got besides Charlie.'' Charlie wrote sports, which Clint knew little about and cared less in spite of the fact that he was six foot five and looked like a linebacker. Except for running track, Clint's only brush with sports was what he read in the sports section.

"Okay, I get the hint.''

"Where do I find this princess?''

"Go out county road six about two miles till you come to a pecan grove and a little yellow farm house.''

"Sam Maxey?''

"Yep, his daughter.''

"I don't recall her. What is she, former homecoming queen?''

"Nope, church secretary.''

"This ought to be good.''

"Play it up, Clint. Make it a feature. I want you to cover her all the way to the state pageant.''

"What about crime? What about obituaries?''

"If anybody kicks the bucket or takes a notion to steal a cow, I'll write about it myself. You get out there and bust your butt over the princess.''

"Thanks, Wayne. You're all heart.''

C.J.'s transformation began with a new hairstyle. Ellie had gone with her to the Kut 'N Kurl. "For moral support,'' she'd said. Three hours and endless torture later, they were back home.

As C.J. stared at herself in the mirror she decided she looked like something that needed a transfusion.

What had once been a perfectly nice head of sleek brown hair now resembled a cow pile, a tall about-to-topple one.

"All I need is pointed fingernails and a long black dress and I'd look like Morticia on *The Addams Family*," she told Ellie.

"Well, it's not exactly what I'd envisioned," Ellie admitted. "I think the perm's a little tight."

"What about this makeup?" The Kut 'N Kurl sold makeup on the side, and their resident expert had *done* C.J.'s face. "I look like yesterday's leftovers that somebody tried to garnish."

"Maybe the lipstick is too red. And, I don't know, the cheeks…"

"Look like stop signs." C.J. grabbed a washcloth and started scrubbing just as the doorbell rang. "Would you get that, Ellie?"

Hearing an unfamiliar deep male voice, C.J. peeked around the bathroom door. Standing in the hall with Ellie was the best-looking man she'd ever seen, on screen or off. To top it off, he looked as if he could lift a small bull without blinking an eye, plus he had longish thick black hair that just begged to be tousled and eyes so blue they didn't look real.

C.J. ducked back inside, caught a glimpse of herself and nearly screamed. All she needed was a wart on her nose and a tall pointy hat to make her transformation complete.

"Is Miss Maxey here?"

Tell him no, C.J. silently screamed. "Yes," Ellie said, and the gorgeous hunk said, "Could I please speak with her? I'm Clint Garrett from the *Tribune*. I've come to interview her."

"I'll go tell her."

C.J. was going to die. She was still the same plain girl she'd always been, but before this morning's ill-fated journey to the Kut 'N Kurl, at least she'd had nice hair. Furthermore, hives were popping out all over her face. Probably from the makeup they'd shoveled on.

"I can't go out there looking like this," she told Ellie.

"What do you want me to tell him?"

"Tell him I'm sick, tell him I've gone to Mars."

"The publicity would be good for the pageant."

"Look at me, Ellie. I look like something the cat dragged up."

"Maybe you could wear a scarf, and, I don't know...pat some cream on the red bumps."

"Maybe I could cover my head with a paper sack."

"Well, we have to tell him something."

C.J. could tell Ellie was disappointed. After all, promoting the dairy princess pageant was part of her job. The least C.J. could do was cooperate.

"Look, tell him I'm coming down with something. Tell him if he'll stand out there in the hall I'll answer his questions."

"I'll see what he says." As Ellie left, C.J. glanced out the bathroom window. The drop-dead gorgeous reporter was riding a Harley. It figured.

"That's an unusual request," Clint said. *Preposterous* was more like it, but he softened his opinion because Ellie seemed like such a nice woman. A little like his mother, plain and sturdy, no frills, face full of character.

"I tried to talk her into coming out, but this is the best I can do. C.J. can be stubborn at times."

"Okay, then. I'll just pull up a chair and shout at her through the bathroom door."

Clint followed along behind and didn't make any bones about eavesdropping when Ellie slipped into the bathroom.

"What did he say?" Nice voice, he decided, definitely the dairy princess. Unless they had a whole gang of women stashed in the bathroom.

"He said okay. I wish you'd come out. He has a killer smile."

Clint chuckled. He'd heard that before, but never from an older woman.

"I don't care if he has a gold-plated you-know-what, I'm not letting him see me like this."

She probably hadn't put on her eye makeup yet. Beauty queens were like that. That's just what he needed, another egomaniac beauty to follow around.

Furthermore, she probably had a bunch of silly, pat answers she would give no matter what he asked…unless he got her off balance first. Then he could take charge and do a *real* interview even if it was only about a local cow queen for a podunk weekly.

Ellie came out of the bathroom. "I'll make tea while you're interviewing her."

As soon as she was out of earshot, Clint drawled, "It's not gold-plated, Miss Maxey, but a few women have called it gilded." He heard strangling sounds in the bathroom. "Miss Maxey, is everything all right in there?"

"Just fine, Mr. Garrett."

''You can call me Clint.''

''Not Sir Clint the Gilded?''

She was fast on her feet. Tart-tongued, too. He liked that. Most women were trying so hard to impress him they wouldn't risk being a smart-mouth. Maybe he'd found a rarity, a beauty queen who wasn't a plastic Barbie doll.

''Only in the bedroom, princess.'' That shut her up. ''How old are you, Miss Maxey?''

''I don't consider that a relevant question. Furthermore, I never trust a woman who tells her age or her weight.''

''Strike that question. How tall are you?''

''Five ten.''

''In three-inch heels?''

''No. In size-nine flat feet.''

''Dress size?''

''Are you going shopping for me, Mr. Garrett?''

''I hadn't planned on it.''

''Then you don't need to know.''

''I guess I can figure that out when I see you in a swimsuit.''

''The dairy princess contest is not that kind of pageant, and I don't plan on going swimming with you, Mr. Garrett.''

Clint hadn't been this entertained in a long time. He decided to goad her a little, see what she would do. ''I interviewed some women up in Tupelo once who called themselves Kuties of the Kudzu Kourt.''

Was she laughing? He enjoyed people who had a sense of humor. Maybe this job of covering the dairy princess wouldn't be that bad after all.

"They all wore hot pants," he added. "Does the dairy princess wear hot pants?"

"Only in the bedroom, Mr. Garrett."

"Touché, Miss Maxey. Your point."

"Is this a contest? I thought it was an interview. What kind of reporter are you?"

"Not much of one, but I'm all you've got. I've been assigned to *cover* you, Miss Maxey."

Silence. Good. He'd finally got the best of her.

"So far you're not doing very well," she said.

"Why don't you come out here and tell me how? Better yet, you can *show* me."

"I wouldn't want you to catch what I have."

"I think what you have is a streak of cowardice. I think you're hiding something from me." Dead silence from her side of the door. Bull's-eye. At last he was onto something. "What is it you're hiding, Miss Maxey?"

"Nothing. I'm completely open."

"Then be warned...I'm fixing to plunge right in."

Chapter Two

Erotic images spun through C.J.'s mind. Good grief, what kind of dairy princess was she? Certainly not the kind to make Ellie proud. If C.J. didn't get her act together she would not only make a fool of herself but of the terrific woman who was like a mother to her.

She had to quit fooling around being a smart-mouth, and give Clint Garrett what he'd come for. She had to lie.

She took several deep steadying breaths.

"Miss Maxey? Are you all right in there?"

"Just a little light-headed."

The door rattled. Good lord, he was trying to come in.

"Unlock the door so I can come in."

"Why?"

"To put a wet washcloth on your head."

"No, I can do that."

Shoot, what next? Tell a little lie, and it leads to all kinds of complications. C.J. turned on the water and let it run awhile.

"I'm okay now," she said.

"You sure? I know my way around a swooning woman."

"I'll just bet you do."

"You sound mighty feisty for somebody sick."

"I'm getting over it." And getting darned tired of the bathroom. C.J. was slightly claustrophobic. "What's your next question, Mr. Garrett?"

"Tell me, what's your platform?"

"I don't have one. I'm not a politician."

"I thought all beauty queens had platforms."

There. She'd done it again. Ellie was going to wish she'd never seen C.J., let alone entrusted her with a title.

"Oh, well, yes, that. My platform is…"

C.J. was stumped. What on earth did beauty queens talk about? The only pageant she'd ever watched was the Miss America pageant five years ago with her friend Sandi.

Clint Garrett tapped on the door. "Miss Maxey…"

"World peace," she shouted.

"What?"

"That's it. My platform is world peace."

"Innovative," he drawled. "May I quote you?"

"By all means."

"Tell me, Miss Maxey. How do you intend to achieve that goal?"

Boy, there was more to being a princess than she'd

imagined. "When I'm riding around in convertibles in parades, I'll smile a lot to spread the peace in my own heart to the crowds. They can pass it on. If everybody does that, pretty soon peace will circle the globe."

"Impressive."

She deserved his sarcasm. Maybe she could buy up all the *Tribunes* so Ellie wouldn't be mortified.

"I need to take pictures," he said.

"What?"

"You know, pictures. To go with the story."

She could imagine it, her looking like a porcupine and the whole town laughing. Her daddy would be disgraced. Not to mention Ellie.

"I'm not up to that today."

"I'll come back tomorrow."

"No, I won't be up to it then, either."

"How do you know?"

"I can tell, that's all."

"How about the day after?"

Was he laughing? At least he had a sense of humor.

"That's Sunday."

"I'll see you in church then."

He would, too. Even through the door she could tell that Clint Garrett was not the kind of man to be put off forever.

"I won't be in church. I'm…going to visit a sick relative." No answer. What fresh hell was he thinking up now? "Mr. Garrett?" Still no response.

"He's gone, C.J.," Ellie said out in the hallway.

"Are you sure?"

"Positive. He came to the kitchen to thank me for the tea. Said he had to rush off to make his deadline."

C.J. heard the unmistakable roar of a motorcycle. "Good." She shoved open the door. "I thought I was never going to get out of here."

"Here. Drink this." C.J. sipped the tea Ellie shoved into her hand. Chamomile. Just what she needed to settle her nerves. "He said he'd be back."

"That's what I'm afraid of."

"Let me take a look at those bumps," Sam said, and C.J. moved into the circle of lamplight so her daddy could see.

"What do you think it is?" She was hoping he'd name something awful that would last six or seven weeks so she could give up her place in the pageant without hurting Ellie's feelings.

This afternoon's interview had been torture. There she was, sitting on the toilet in the small cramped bathroom while that gorgeous hunk goaded her from the other side of the door. It wouldn't be so bad if one interview was all he wanted, but *no,* he was fixing to latch on to her like a duck on a junebug. From now till this fiasco was over, every time she looked up, Clint Garrett would be there.

"It's hives," Sam said. "A little cortisone cream will fix that right up."

C.J. went to dig some out of the medicine cabinet, then she dunked her head under the faucet and shampooed her frizzy hair for the third time. The stylist down at Kut 'N Kurl had warned her not to shampoo for forty-eight hours. "It'll take the curl right out, hon," she'd said.

C.J. sincerely hoped so. With her hair sticking out

every which way she looked like she'd been electrocuted.

Sam stuck his head around the doorjamb. "'Night, C.J. I'm going to bed."

It was only eight o'clock. C.J. wrapped her hair in a towel and followed him down the hall. "Dad, why don't we watch TV together? There's a John Wayne western on The Movie Channel."

"I'm a little tired. Fishing's hard work."

His attempt at lightheartedness didn't work. For all the interest he took in life, Sam Maxey might as well have died with Phoebe six years ago.

A familiar guilt swept over C.J. If only she hadn't wanted to go to the mall in Tupelo that night. If only she hadn't asked to drive. If only she'd been in the passenger side when the car came out of nowhere and smashed into them. Her mother had lived three years after the accident, three long, tortuous years that wiped out their bank account and destroyed their dreams.

Although Sam had told her the accident wasn't her fault, C.J. blamed herself. Phoebe hadn't wanted to go that night. It was raining and she'd wanted to do some baking for the Christmas holidays.

But C.J. had insisted. When you're sixteen, nothing matters more than a new dress for the prom.

The dress was still in C.J.'s closet, her hair shirt she called it, a constant reminder that she'd caused her mother's death.

Was that why she stayed in Hot Coffee? Ellie said it was. Periodically she would say, "C.J., it's time to move on. Sam will be fine without you." But the lure of big cities and bright lights held no appeal for C.J.

All she'd ever wanted to do was get a degree in veterinary medicine and settle down to a small practice in Hot Coffee. But not alone. That was the other part of her dream. She wanted somebody to love. Somebody who would overlook all her flaws and love her right back.

All of a sudden C.J. was so lonely she could die. Here it was, Friday night and she was by herself in a chenille robe with a torn pocket. She picked up the phone and called Sandi for all the good it would do. Even in a town as small as Hot Coffee Sandi was always the center of a social whirl.

Sandi answered on the first ring.

"Want to come over and watch TV?" C.J. asked her friend. "There's a good steamy classic coming on. Farley Granger and Lana Turner."

"Sure. And you can tell me more about this dairy princess thing."

"Arrgh!"

"It can't be that bad."

"It's worse," C.J. insisted.

"I'll be right there. Got any popcorn?"

"Plenty."

C.J. flipped on the porch light, and within minutes Sandi emerged from the hedge that bordered their properties.

"What did they do to you?" she said the minute she saw C.J.'s wet, frizzled hair.

"I wanted to wait about going to the beauty shop till you got back from Jackson to supervise, but I didn't want to hurt Ellie's feelings."

Sandi patted C.J.'s hair this way and that, studying it with a critical eye. She was an artist with both camera and brush, highly sought-after as both a professional photographer and a portrait painter. She'd just returned from the state's capitol where she'd photographed a society wedding.

"I think I can fix it. Do you have any scissors?"

C.J. fetched them from the kitchen, and they watched the movie while Sandi snipped.

"I just love this part," C.J. said, and they fell silent while Lana Turner walked into the room wearing a bathrobe and a towel on her head.

"Nobody looks that good with a towel on her head," Sandi said.

"You do."

"Don't I wish." Sandi put down the scissors. "There now. When that dries, just fluff it up with your fingertips. How about that popcorn?"

They made a big bowlful and had just settled down when a Harley roared up the driveway.

"Good lord, what is that?" Sandi said.

"The *Tribune*'s ace reporter chasing Hot Coffee's hottest story."

"You mean…the dairy princess?"

"Yes." C.J. raced to the window while Sandi burst into giggles. "It's not funny." Clint Garrett in the moonlight in a helmet was a sight to see. A mouth-watering morsel she'd stand and drool over if she didn't have to hide.

He was already coming up the sidewalk. Any minute now he'd be ringing the bell, then he'd be inside, in the living breathing flesh. If he saw her like this she'd be humiliated.

"Quick, Sandi. Stall him." She streaked by her

friend toward the hall, then backtracked for the pop-corn. No sense suffering starvation, too.

"What will I say?"

"I don't know. Anything. Just don't let him know I'm here."

"Okay. But you can't hide forever, you know."

"Maybe till I'm thirty and a kindly godmother sprinkles me with fairy dust."

"C.J., you have lots going for you," Sandi said, but C.J. didn't stop to argue. This was war and the enemy was at the door. "All's fair," she yelled as she took the coward's way out.

Clint was counting on the element of surprise. He hadn't believed for a minute that Miss C. J. Maxey was sick, and he was here to prove it. Not only that, he was here to get answers. Real ones. Pictures, too.

Maybe he wasn't with the *Washington Post,* but he had his pride.

He rang the doorbell. The princess was probably in there thinking up ways to avoid him. He was getting ready to press it again when the door swung open and revealed the most beautiful creature in the world. A real knockout. A blond bombshell with a pinup's body and a face that belonged on the movie screen.

This was too good to be true. Why the hell had she hid in the bathroom? Obviously she'd been sick after all.

"Are you contagious?" he said.

"My third fiancé thought so." Her smile lit up the whole countryside. Funny, though, he didn't feel a thing. The dairy princess wasn't nearly as exciting in person as she had been hiding in the bathroom sending barbs through the door.

"You're engaged?" He thought that was against the rules.

"No, not currently. Won't you come in?"

C.J. had never thought of herself as the kind of person who would eavesdrop, but here she was standing behind the door in a darkened hallway peeking through the crack while her best friend in the whole world charmed the greatest-looking man who had ever set foot in C.J.'s house.

Why did it have to be this way? Why couldn't she be the one on the sofa making Clint Garrett laugh instead of cowering behind the door like a wet chicken?

She'd never considered herself the kind of woman given over to envy, but here she was turning green. Furthermore, from the looks of things it wouldn't be long before Clint Garrett joined the long list of men besotted with Sandi.

Not that it was Sandi's fault. She just naturally attracted men, that's all. Besides, she was merely doing what C.J. had asked. She didn't have a clue that Hot Coffee's ace reporter was anything to C.J. except a nuisance.

And he wasn't. Not really. It was just that C.J.'s breathing felt funny and she had a sudden urge to rush into the room and yell "STOP!"

Stop what, for Pete's sake? Sandi and Clint weren't doing anything.

Yet.

C.J. hated that sarcastic little voice in her head.

She'd show it who was boss. Taking her bowl of popcorn she went into the bathroom with the full intention of eating every last morsel.

She dug in, certain the salty buttery taste would make her forget what was going on in her living room.

"Nothing's going on," she snapped, then she bolted off the toilet seat, wrapped a towel around her still-wet hair, smeared a ton of cream on her face, tightened the belt on her tacky chenille robe and marched into the den, blue fuzzy house shoes and all.

"Hello, there." Her announcement startled them.

Sandi put a hand over her mouth to stop a gale of giggles.

"I suppose you came to see me," C.J. said.

"Yes, as a matter of fact, I did."

"Well, here I am."

The space between the door and the sofa looked a million miles long, a desert as vast as the Sahara that she had to cross while he watched. How did Lana do it with that towel on her head?

C.J. affected a beauty queen walk, something half-way between a seductive slither and a minx's mince. Clint grinned. It had to be the shoes. They hampered her style.

"I really hate to miss this, but I have to be going."

"Must you, Sandi?" C.J. tried for a royal murmur, but the cold cream spoiled the effect. "I'll see you to the door."

Anything for a brief respite from the disturbing Mr. Garrett.

"Call me," Sandi whispered when they got to the

door, and C.J. nodded. Numb, that's how she felt. She
might never get over it.

She stood at the door watching until Sandi was
safely through the hedge. Then she kept her back to
the room because she was afraid to turn around.
Whatever had possessed her to come out of hiding?
Obviously she was going crazy. She'd be the only
princess in the state of Mississippi carted off to Whit-
field in a padded truck.

"Crystal Jean?"

C.J. whirled around. "How did you know my real
name?"

"Sandi told me."

"What else did she tell you?"

"I think it's much more fun to keep you guessing."

If he was trying to throw her off balance again, it
wasn't going to work. Men like Clint Garrett were far
too dangerous to risk losing control.

"It's late." Abandoning queenly behavior altogether, C.J. stalked to the sofa and plopped down.

He grinned. "I know. Did I catch you at a bad
time?"

"Yes, you caught me in the middle of a beauty
ritual."

"Do you do this ritual often?"

"Every night. Faithfully. I'm thinking of going
public with my beauty secrets."

She wished she wouldn't do that, revert to sarcasm
when she was uncertain, but she couldn't help herself.
It was a handy weapon for keeping people at bay. Not
that they wanted to be any other way with C.J., par-
ticularly good-looking men. What she ought to do
was learn some trick for drawing them closer.

"I'm sure they're waiting with bated breath." He sniffed. "Do I smell popcorn?"

"Yes."

"Why don't we share? I've always liked eating popcorn from the same bowl as a beauty queen."

She didn't miss the devilish glint in his eyes. "I'll get it."

Why not? She couldn't toss him out: he was too big. And besides, it would be her one and only chance to spend Friday night watching a romantic movie with a heartthrob.

While she was pretending to be a princess, she might as well enjoy the benefits. It beat working late typing church bulletins.

When she walked in with the popcorn, Clint grinned and patted the sofa.

"I saved a warm spot for you."

Up close he was gorgeous and absolutely irresistible. When she sat down her robe slid open as if she'd planned it that way, like a seduction by Lana Turner. Instead of grabbing it like a schoolgirl, C.J. decided that for once in her life she'd be bold, she'd be a real seductress. After all, she had her hands full with the popcorn bowl, and besides, when would she ever get another chance at glamour and excess?

"Nice legs," he said.

"Thanks."

Clint didn't make any bones about it: he stared. If the rest of her looked as good as the enticing bit he was seeing, she'd win the pageant hands down.

"Want some popcorn?" She was all business as she shoved the bowl at him. It was the damnedest thing he'd ever seen, a beauty queen without artifice, without a feminine wile to her name.

Somebody must have told her in advance about him. Wayne, maybe. He must have told her that nothing worked better with Clint Garrett than total lack of interest.

So what if C. J. Maxey was feigning the whole thing? It was working.

"I'll hold the bowl while you take off your beauty mask."

She sized him up with a killer pair of eyes that more than matched her killer legs, eyes that were the stuff poets write about. They were big as dinner plates, and so deep blue they looked navy.

"It has to set," she said.

"Pardon?"

She gave him a satisfied cat's smile. She knew she'd scored, darn her delicious hide.

"The beauty cream. It has to set."

"In that case, you hold the bowl and I'll do the honors."

"The honors?"

"Yes." He grabbed a handful of buttery morsels and held them to her lips. Big, soft, sensual-looking lips that all of a sudden he wanted to kiss. He would have if she'd been any other woman, but in spite of the cold cream and the towel on her head, there was something about C. J. Maxey that demanded respect, a quiet dignity that gave him pause.

Clint was no monk, not by a long shot. He'd had his share of flings, but that's all they'd been, brief romps with women no more interested in attachments than he.

But this was different. C.J. was a wild card, someone completely unknown to him. Warning bells clanged and stoplights flashed. Until he knew that she wasn't the kind of woman who played for keeps, he would rein in his appetites, put a lid on his libido and do the smart thing: get the story and leave.

"Hmm, delicious," she said, then licked the butter off her lips.

Clint nearly came unhinged. He was glad he wasn't planning on moving for the next hour or two because in his present state movement would be awkward if not downright painful.

He was going to kill Wayne when he saw him. But first he was going to get what he'd come for…a face-to-face interview that would reveal the *real* C. J. Maxey.

He was trying to think of a great opening ploy when the indomitable Miss Maxey said, "Did you come here to interview me or to stare?"

Caught redhanded. Clint jumped up as if the sofa had burst into flames. "Gotta stretch my legs." She gave him a satisfied smile.

Why hadn't he gone to Al's pool hall, had a few beers, played a little pool, then gone on home and settled down with a horror story? Stephen King was a lot less dangerous than C. J. Maxey.

"I guess your lifelong ambition has been to wear a beauty crown?" *Great.* The perfect opening question. Required a one-word answer. It was too late to take it back. He'd have to do better next time.

"No," she said.

"No?"

"That's what I said."

He'd thought all beauty queens were talkative. Ask them something that required *yes* or *no* and they'd go on for fifteen minutes about their vision for saving the world.

"Why do you want to be Mississippi's Dairy Princess?"

"Greed," she deadpanned, but her eyes gave her away. They sparkled with malicious glee.

"Do you expect the title to catapult you to fame and fortune and a rich husband?"

"Rich *and* good-looking. It wouldn't hurt if he's also gold-plated."

She was putting him on. But why? He was going to find out, even if he had to play dirty. Making no bones about staring, Clint moved in and leaned down till he was nose to nose with her.

"May I quote you on that, Miss Maxey?"

C.J. nearly upended the popcorn bowl. Ellie was going to kill her, plain and simple. Here she was supposed to represent the dairy interests of Lee County as well as give Ellie a good name among county agents, and all she could do was poke out her stinger. And all because Clint Garrett was tanned and muscular, six foot five if he was an inch, and every inch of him lip-smacking good.

Why couldn't she be the kind of woman who seduced men on sofas instead of the kind of woman who reduced men to boredom? Why couldn't she be a natural glamour puss instead of a plain country girl hiding behind five pounds of cold cream?

She leaned as far back as she could, but he was still so close she could smell the soap he'd used.

Instead, she drew herself up tall and relied on her brain.

"No, Mr. Garrett. You may not. You may leave."

"Leave?"

"Yes. Due to your unprofessional conduct, this interview is over."

C.J. left him sitting on the sofa. It was her best queenly exit.

Chapter Three

The two ceiling fans in the *Tribune*'s office did nothing but stir up the muggy air and send a few flyers for the Shriner's upcoming circus fluttering to the floor. Clint and Wayne leaned back in matching swivel chairs—both were equally ratty—with their feet propped on Wayne's desk.

A big pitcher of cold lemonade sat on the desk between them making water circles on the already much-abused desk, and from time to time one of them reached over and refilled their glasses. A copy of the *Tribune* lay open to Clint's story on the dairy princess.

"I thought you'd get pictures," Wayne said.

"She hid behind the bathroom door the first time I interviewed her and behind a truck-load of cold cream the next."

Clint got lost in thought remembering the narrow escape he'd had from the dairy princess Friday night. If that robe of hers had edged open one more inch he'd have had his wicked way with her on the sofa, cold cream or no cold cream.

"I even went to church trying to get a picture, but she didn't show up," he added.

Wayne grunted. "Maybe you can catch her at work."

"That's kind of boring, don't you think?" He made a frame with his hands. "Dairy Princess Types."

"Yeah. I see what you mean."

Eyeing the flyers on the floor, Clint grinned. "I was thinking of something far more exciting for Miss Crystal Jean Maxey." His brain was cooking with ideas of parades and revels with Miss C. J. Maxey as star of the show.

"What sort of devilment are you up to now?"

"Wouldn't you rather be surprised?"

"Yeah. It's safer that way. When the sheriff comes to question me I can always claim ignorance."

C.J.'s support team was gathered in her living room for a summit conference…Sam, Ellie, Sandi. Ellie had brought cookies, Sam supplied the cola and Sandi had brought a twelve-pack of Hershey's candy bars with almonds.

Sam had made a huge dent in the cookies while C.J. and Sandi had plowed through the chocolate.

The candy hadn't helped one bit. In spite of the fact that her rash had cleared and her hair looked bet-

ter than it ever had, C.J. was still panicked at the
thought of her first official public appearance.

"What am I going to do?" she said.

"You'll do just fine." Ellie adjusted the straps on
C.J.'s simple yellow sundress. "It's only a parade."

"A *circus* parade."

"You've always loved animals," Sam said.

She had. And if it were only tigers and lions she
had to worry about, everything would be all right. But
there was one animal she hadn't counted on…Clint
Garrett. According to the Shriner who had called, the
Tribune's ace reporter would be on the float with her.

"All you have to do is wave." Sandi reached for
another candy bar, and Ellie said, "Good lord, where
do you put it all?"

"Stress eating," Sandi said.

"What are you stressed about?" C.J. asked.
"You're not the one stuck in the middle of a circus
parade behind the elephants!"

"Better you than me." Ellie fanned herself with
the *Tribune*. "Good lord, it's hot."

"It's cooler on the porch," Sam said.

"Let's go." Ellie hugged C.J. "You'll be just fine.
Sam and I will be on the sidelines cheering you on.
Now, show me that beauty queen's wave."

C.J. flapped her hand, limp at the wrist. "You've
got it down pat," Ellie said, then followed Sam out.

"Shoot," C.J. said. "I'm so depressed I could cry.
I'm going to make a fool of myself."

"No, you're not." Sandi shoved the remains of
their food binge aside. "You're going to be the star
of the show." She unzipped the duffel bag she'd

brought and pulled out a red sequined gown. "I brought you a little something."

It was a beautiful gown, designer label, bought in Paris. C.J. had seen Sandi wear it once. It showcased Sandi's dynamite figure to a tee, but C.J. was shaped more like a firecracker. Straight up and down. Without the fuse.

But how could she refuse the gown without hurting Sandi's feelings?

"That's very generous of you, but I can't possibly wear something this fine in a circus parade."

"Of course you can."

"I'll sweat on it."

"André spilled a whole bottle of champagne on it once." Was he Sandi's first fiancé or her second? C.J. couldn't keep them straight. Sandi held the gown in front of her. "It's going to look great."

"On you, maybe, but I don't think I'll fill it up."

"I guarantee you will." Sandi reached into the bag once more. "They don't call these things WonderBras for nothing."

Clint was late. He'd got behind a funeral procession and had to poke along at fifteen miles an hour. Parade or no parade, there was no way he could pull out and roar past a hearse with an escort of half the sheriff's department. The law of Hot Coffee didn't take kindly to disrespect.

When the deceased's entourage finally pulled into the gravel lane that led to Our Lady of the Sorrows Church, Clint kicked his Harley into life and raced toward the fairgrounds in search of Crystal Jean Maxey.

Today she had no place to hide. What would she look like? He hadn't been this excited since he was six years old and waiting for a Christmas puppy.

The fairgrounds on Main Street teemed with life— convertibles and floats draped with crepe paper vied for space with prancing Arabians and restless caged tigers. Clint slowed to a crawl, craning his neck for a glimpse of the dairy princess. Her float was just up ahead waiting in front of the building where every fall the homemakers of Hot Coffee displayed their pies and cakes and pickled peaches at the county fair.

Hundreds of crepe paper roses adorned Leonard Lumpkin's flatbed truck. That had to be Leonard himself standing beside the cab awaiting the honor of driving the princess in her first parade. His hair was slicked back in a greasy ducktail, his red shirt was ringed with sweat and his Adam's apple bulged above a necktie that featured Mickey Mouse.

Any man who would wear a tie like that couldn't be bad. Clint parked his motorbike and was fixing to give Leonard a hearty handshake when this foxy chick dressed in red slithered up and changed his mind about everything he'd ever thought.

One, Leonard was obviously a pervert because he suddenly grew six hands, every one of them patting the princess in places they had no business being. Two, the princess herself was not refreshingly different after all. She was merely another Barbie doll with cleavage stuck out halfway to Texas and a rounded woman's butt just begging to be pinched. Which was exactly what Leonard was trying to do.

The princess sidestepped so fast her banner got

crooked. But for all her pretense of modesty, she gave Leonard a smile designed to dazzle and seduce.

Clint was speechless with rage, but what took him most by surprise was his disappointment. C. J. Maxey had played him for a fool. She'd led him on with her sharp wit and her pretense of guilelessness. She'd made him think that behind all that cold cream was a woman with a brain in her head. Somebody he could enjoy talking with. Shoot, she might even have turned out to be destiny's final joke on him—a woman who could make him straighten up and fly right, a woman who could make him believe in himself.

Instead she was just another shallow flirt.

She had a dazzling smile beamed on Leonard, and clearly he was completely fooled by her act. But she couldn't fool Clint. Nosirree. Women like her were a dime a dozen. He had them for breakfast. He chewed them up then spit them out.

Which was exactly what he was fixing to do with Miss Crystal Jean Maxey. Actually, he ought to be grateful to her for flaunting her wares. She'd saved him from departing the familiar routine that had worked for him for years. Love 'em and leave 'em. Trite but true. Well, almost. Everything except the *love* part. There wasn't a bit of feeling involved in his brief encounters with women, which made it easy for Clint to keep on drifting.

C.J. outmatched poor Leonard, but that wouldn't be a problem with Clint. The way he figured it, he and C. J. Maxey deserved each other, the worthless bastard and the shameless tease.

Just as Leonard was fixing to boost C.J. onto the

back of his flatbed truck, Clint stalked over and plucked her out of his hands.

"Allow me."

C.J. gave a little squawk of surprise, and Leonard said, "Well, I beg your pardon."

Clint ignored both of them and let nature take its course. Her skirt had a side slit and his hand was right there. He ran it down the length of one long slender, silky leg.

"What do you think you're doing?" C.J. said.

"Yeah, just what the hell do you think you're doing?" Leonard stuck out his jaw and strutted around like a turkey cock.

"My job."

For a moment Leonard looked as if he might take umbrage, then he climbed into the cab of his truck and slammed the door.

In a big show of false modesty, C.J. *did* take umbrage. "Your *job?*"

"Yes, I'm your escort for the day."

His laugh was decidedly hollow. Even with all her inexperience, C.J. could see that. When he pulled her against his chest with a soft whump, he held her so tight her push-up pads almost popped out. C.J. had never been so mortified in her whole life...nor so thrilled.

She was actually *wallowing* in the arms of a handsome hunk. She didn't know what she'd been missing. All those lonely dreams she'd had about being in the arms of a man paled by comparison to the real thing.

Not that he was doing anything except boosting her onto the float. Still, this newfound sexual power was heady stuff. All she'd had to do was pad herself within an inch of her life and bat her eyelashes.

She didn't want to think about how shallow that made her…as well as him. She was just going to enjoy her fleeting moment as a vamp.

What would a vamp do in a situation like this? *Think,* she ordered herself. *You're the one with the brain.*

"My, what *big* muscles you have."

She'd meant to sound sexy instead of scared, but he didn't seem to notice. Nor did he notice how her hands trembled when she ran them over his broad chest. She saw an enticing glimpse of chest hair and was tempted to delve inside his shirt, but instead erred on the side of caution. She wanted him to think she was sophisticated and sexy. A panic attack would spoil the effect.

"You should see them up close and personal."

"I plan to."

C.J. actually licked her lips. He'd think she was an idiot. But no, he watched as if he'd never seen anything more fascinating than her tongue.

"I wouldn't do that again if I were you, princess."

"Why not?"

"The dairy barn is just around the corner." He lifted one eyebrow which gave him a devilish look and her another panic attack. "All those haystacks."

His voice vibrated through her like a bass kettle drum. Every inch of her caught fire—her skin, her bones, her blood. Lord, what would she do if he kidnapped her and took her to one of those haystacks? Her heart hammered so hard she was sure he'd see what a fraud she was.

Shoot, she didn't want the game to end. "Promises, promises," she murmured.

He bent so close she thought he was going to kiss her. Lord, she'd scream. She'd swoon. She'd die. She squeezed her eyes shut and parted her lips.

"Save the pucker, Crystal Jean. It's party time."

He plopped her unceremoniously onto the flatbed truck, then climbed in behind her and strolled toward her throne as if nothing unusual had happened. Meanwhile she sat on the hay-littered flatbed with a dusty bottom and a bruised ego.

"Better climb onto your throne, princess. The parade's about to start."

Ignoring her outstretched hand he made a big to-do of plumping up the red velvet seat cushion on her throne. Up front Leonard revved the motor and in the distance animals snarled while their trainers yelled commands.

C.J. picked herself up, gathered the remnants of her dignity and walked toward her throne in a manner that would have been regal except the bits of hay clinging to Sandi's sequined gown spoiled the effect.

As she breezed by Clint she snapped, "You're no gentleman."

"That makes us a matched set." He plucked the hay off her gown, then swatted her bottom. "You're no lady."

Oh help. Now what had she done? Every time she set out to be something she wasn't, the ploy backfired. You'd think she'd learn. The only problem was, it was so much more fun being something besides plain, boring C. J. Maxey, the church secretary.

* * *

The truck lurched and C.J.'s banner slid one way, her crown the other. She sat down in the nick of time, otherwise she'd have sailed over the top of Leonard's cab and smack into the rump of the elephant bringing up the rear of the pachyderm parade.

"You look right at home on a throne." Clint strolled to the front end of the flatbed as if the truck were not pitching and rolling over bumpy asphalt.

C.J. thought she looked ridiculous, but she didn't say so. She'd made up her mind to curb her tongue for Ellie's sake. Just for a few weeks...until the pageant was over. Then she'd go back to being her old acerbic self.

"Give me that royal smile," Clint said, and she grimaced for the camera while the shutter clicked. She hated this. All of it. The posturing and preening, the gaudy public display, the tacky spray-painted throne. Everything except the chance for a heady flirtation just like an ordinary girl.

"Look, there she is," Ellie yelled. She and Sandi and Sam were under the awning of Wright's Drugstore wearing sun visors and eating ice cream.

"You look mighty fine," Sam hollered, and suddenly C.J. became one of the characters in her favorite childhood stories. Her heart filled with such love and joy she figured it was at least two sizes bigger.

Okay, so she didn't hate everything about being princess. She'd gladly suffer a few indignities if she could make Sam smile.

"Your dad?" Clint asked, and when C.J. nodded he waved, but his smile was directed mostly at Sandi.

The green-eyed monster tweaked C.J., and she was ashamed of herself. She decided it was easier to be sweet when you're plain and nobody ever looks at you anyhow. Put on padding and too much lipstick and all of a sudden you're somebody even you don't like.

No wonder Clint was craning his neck to get one last glimpse of Sandi. *Forget it,* C.J. told herself, then applied her newly acquired royal waving skills to the crowd. It looked as if everybody in Hot Coffee had turned out for the parade. Not that C.J. took any credit. It was the exotic animals, the clowns, the be-spangled trapeze artists that folks came to see.

If C.J. had been planning the parade she'd have put the circus up front with her own float trailing along behind instead of smack in the middle. Being behind the elephants had distinct disadvantages. For one thing there was no way Leonard could see around several tons of pachyderm.

All of a sudden the truck lurched left and Clint said, "This is not the parade route. What does that fool think he's doing?"

"Following the elephants."

"The elephants are going the wrong way."

"Perhaps you'd like to get out and argue with them."

There. Her stinger was back. Maybe her sanity, too. She was fed up with pretense.

Behind them the prancing horses made the turn, followed by the caged lions and tigers, fifteen clowns in the trick clown car and the brass band blaring "Seventy-six Trombones."

"The whole parade is going the wrong way." Clint rapped on the back window of the cab, but Leonard ignored him. "Stop," he shouted. "You've got to turn this truck around."

But Leonard kept on driving.

"I don't think he hears you. Either that or he's getting his revenge." C.J. laughed. "It must be so sweet."

"He's going to think revenge."

"What diabolical plot are you hatching now?"

He lifted one devilish eyebrow that shot her temperature up ten degrees. "You think I'm diabolical?"

"Among other things."

"What other things?"

Up front a huge commotion cut off the lie C.J. was fixing to tell. People yelled, sirens screamed and Leonard screeched to such an abrupt stop, she toppled off her throne.

Clint knelt beside her and helped her up. "Are you all right?"

She barely had time to say *yes* before two Arabian horses streaked by followed by trainers hollering, "Whoa, whoa boy." The horses galloped into the midst of the elephants who started trumpeting their alarm. The one bringing up the rear backed into the front of Leonard's truck which sent C.J. crashing straight into Clint's arms.

Was she imagining things, or did he caress her softly before scooping her up?

"What are you doing?"

"Getting you out of here."

"Why?"

He didn't answer until he'd got her safely off the truck. "Look at the intersection up ahead."

On one side of the intersection cops milled around

their motorcycles tooting their whistles and waving their arms while on the other side, people wearing their Sunday best bailed out of their cars shouting and craning their necks. Where the streets converged the elephants lumbered round and round with their chains rattling and their owners shouting commands. And in the midst of it all sat a long black hearse.

"Good grief," C.J. said.

"That's right. The elephants crashed through a funeral procession." Clint practically dragged C.J. to the top of a grassy slope that overlooked the cemetery.

"You should be safe here," he said, then took off running.

"What are you going to do?" she shouted, but he didn't answer.

What did he think she was? Some hothouse flower? She wasn't about to miss the most excitement Hot Coffee had seen since a sore loser turned a skunk loose at the postmistress's wedding.

As she descended the slope the brass band started playing "Amazing Grace." Somebody must have told them the parade had crashed a funeral procession. The haunting strains fell over the melee like a warm cozy blanket. A hush fell over the crowd, and the animals began to settle back into line.

C.J. skirted the clowns and made a beeline for the woman in black standing outside a Lincoln Continental. Petite and gray-haired, she lifted the veil on her hat and shaded her eyes as she peered toward the elephants.

"Mrs. Lars! I had no idea." C.J. squeezed the hand Doris Lars offered.

"Crystal Jean." Her hand fluttered to her mouth. "I was trying to see Lars." She cast a glance toward the hearse still held captive by the circle of marching elephants.

"I'm so sorry. How terrible for you."

The bereaved widow smiled at her. "Oh, no. There's nothing Lars loved more than a parade. He'd be tickled pink to know his last journey on this earth was right in the middle of one. I couldn't have planned it better myself."

"That's a relief. I'd hate to know I was part of something that added to your grief."

"Oh, no, dear. That nice man told the band to play Lars's favorite song."

"What nice young man?"

Doris nodded toward a tall, broad-shouldered man who was helping lift a big cat wagon with a broken axle.

"Clint Garrett?" Who would have thought he'd have a chivalrous bone in his body.

"Yes, he's the one. He said he'd get the band to play at the graveside if I wanted to. Isn't he nice?"

Nice was hardly the word she'd use to describe him. Still, sometimes people rose to the occasion.

"He surely is." She'd told so many lies, what did one more hurt? "Is there anything I can do for you, Mrs. Lars?"

"Well, dear, it would be lovely if you and that nice young man would come to the graveside services."

C.J. looked down at herself. "This dress..."

"It's perfectly wonderful. I always thought people should wear party clothes to funerals. To celebrate a homecoming, you know. The only reason I'm in black is Lars's mother. Poor dear, she'd never speak to me again.''

C.J. glanced into the Lincoln at a stooped woman with a hearing aid and a cane. She had a black shawl draped over her shoulders in spite of the ninety-degree heat.

''I wouldn't want to upset her.''

''Here, dear, put this on.'' Doris pulled off her linen suit jacket and draped it over C.J.'s shoulders. ''Now go fetch that young man. It looks like the elephants are moving.''

Chapter Four

A sense of unease nagged at Clint and he glanced toward the top of the hill to see if he could spot C.J. She was nowhere in sight.

"Damn!" His anxiety ratcheted up a notch. He wasn't accustomed to worrying about anybody, and he didn't like it. He felt as if tentacles were wrapping around him, smothering him.

"Heave," the man at the head of the wagon yelled, and Clint put his shoulder to the task. C.J. could take care of herself. She was a big girl.

All dressed in red. C. J. Maxey was a magnet that would attract every red-blooded male in the circus. He swore again just as somebody tapped him on the shoulder.

"Clint."

It was C.J., the man-magnet, in spite of the fact that she was now partially covered by a black jacket.

"What do you want?" She jumped back as if he'd slapped her. *Good.* Maybe that would put things back into perspective.

"I came to deliver a message. I'll go tell Mrs. Lars your answer is no."

He motioned a burly clown to take his place at the wagon, then took C.J.'s arm and led her away from the commotion.

"I'll decide the answer for myself. What's the question?"

Her face glowed when she softened, and Clint's insides melted like a toasted marshmallow. "Mrs. Lars wanted to know if you would attend her husband's graveside services."

"Of course."

"Of course?"

"Why does that surprise you?"

"I don't know. I never figured you for the soft type."

"I'm neither soft nor sentimental, and don't you forget it." He came very close to telling her the truth, that he was a man without a heart, but he didn't want to reveal that much of himself to her. The less she knew about him, the better.

"I'll go tell her."

"You do that." She walked off, stiff-backed. "C.J.!"

"What?"

"You be careful."

"Ha!" She whirled around and marched off, mad as any woman he'd ever seen.

Lord, he was lucky not to get involved. Women were nothing but trouble, always wanting to make a man over, tie a noose around his neck and lead him to the altar. He hung around the wagon long enough to get it rolling, then he moved up and down the line, doing what he could till the circus was moving back toward town.

Everything except the band. Clint followed as they headed to Peaceful Valley Cemetery. C.J. was standing beside the widow, stunning in red, the coat clasped tightly around her throat, her short hair ruffling in the breeze that had come up.

She's safe. Something inside Clint settled down. He took several deep breaths, then moved to the opposite side of the grave, away from trouble.

The band struck up a song he remembered from his mother's funeral, "Shall We Gather at the River." An overwhelming sense of loneliness took him by surprise, and he tried to push it back by observing C.J. as she wiped away tears. She was either a good actress or else she had a tender heart. A good actress, he decided. Believing that was the only way he could continue on the course he'd set.

After the services, he paid his respects to the widow, then took C.J.'s arm. "Come with me."

She waited until they were outside the gates, then jerked her arm out of his grasp. "Don't you ever do anything besides give orders?"

He grinned. "Yeah. If you can hold off long enough, I'll show you."

"Hell will freeze over before I'll sleep with you."

"Who said anything about sleeping? I'm going to take you home."

The flush on her cheeks looked genuine. Men were

suckers for blushing maidens with lots of cleavage. Innocence and sensuality. A lethal combination.

"I have my car."

"All right then, I'll take you back to your car."

But not right away. He didn't tell her that, of course. She'd have walked back to town, stubborn, temperamental woman that she was.

No, what he had in mind for C. J. Maxey wouldn't do to tell.

The motorcycle parked half a block from the cemetery screamed *power*. It exuded excitement. It reeked of adventure.

Lord, she'd forgotten about that big Harley hog. Nervous sweat popped out all over her, then trickled down her neck and into her cleavage.

"How did that get here?" she asked.

"Cell phone. I called my editor and he and Charlie brought it over." He retrieved two helmets from the saddlebag, then handed her the smaller one. "Here. Put this on."

"If you think I'm riding that thing, you're crazy."

"I never figured you for a coward."

"I'm not. I just don't like the company, that's all."

"'Fraid you're stuck with me, princess. Unless you want to walk back to town."

It was only a couple of miles. She would have walked if she hadn't been wearing high-heeled shoes and Sandi's dress. She could imagine what it would look like after a two-mile trek in this heat.

From the look on Clint's face, he was ready to leave her behind if she kept being mule-headed. She'd never been on a motorcycle. The idea of riding along behind the town's biggest hunk scared her, but it excited her, too. Thrilled her, actually. All that proximity. Bodies pressed against each other.

"Fine. I'll go with you."

She put the helmet on and struggled with straps and fastenings and earphones. Clint watched long enough to make her want to scream, then without a word stepped over and fixed it for her. He took his sweet time, too.

"Wait right there. I'll get on first to steady it, then you climb on behind me." He gave her a wicked grin. "Better lift that skirt out of the way."

"Naturally. I knew that."

It took her a while to get on, mainly because she was trying to preserve a shred of modesty. There was no way she could lift her leg over the Harley without ripping Sandi's dress. In the end, she lifted her skirt to the point of indecency and climbed aboard.

By the time she was seated she felt like she was showing practically everything she had. Even if the helmet did hide most of her face, everybody in town would recognize that red dress. Served her right for parading around pretending to be something she wasn't.

If she'd worn the yellow sundress, she could have looked more like Audrey Hepburn riding behind a hero with her skirt billowing gracefully.

Clint revved the motor. The sound thrilled her all the way to her toes. Here she was doing something dangerous and sexy, and even if it didn't mean a thing to Clint, still it was one of the high points of C.J.'s drab, unexciting life.

"All you have to do is hang on tight and lean in

the same direction I do when we take the curves. I'll try not to scare you."

"I'm not scared of anything."

"All right, then." He peeled out and roared down the road. Trees and houses blurred. C.J. felt airborne; she felt exhilarated; she felt free.

"How're you doing back there?"

"I'm rather enjoying myself." Oh, lord, she sounded like somebody's maiden aunt. "Great," she added.

"Since you're enjoying the ride so much, why don't we take a little spin?"

Why not? Her lifestyle left very little room for spontaneity. Until today she'd never thought how routine can deaden a person, sap the life out, take away the fun.

"It's fine by me," she said, but Clint had already turned onto a country road, leaving the streets and clipped hedges and carefully mowed lawns behind. She should have known a man like Clint wouldn't wait around for permission.

He increased his speed so that it felt as if they were standing still while the landscape floated past. Horses zipped by, and cows chewing cuds. Lakes and haystacks whizzed past, jumbled together so the domes of hay appeared to be rising out of the water.

C.J. tried to imprint everything on her mind so she could remember this day. Always. If she were keeping a scrapbook she'd call it "The Day I Became Real."

She'd never felt more alive. Up until today, she'd been sleepwalking. Now she felt reborn, a woman with ideas and yearnings and passion. The strength of her desire amazed her. She'd known what was missing from her life, but she'd never known its power. Lord, she felt as if she might burst into flames. And that just from riding pressed against the back of Clint. What if she were pressed against the front? C.J. actually groaned.

"Are you all right back there?"

Clint's voice jerked her out of her reverie. "What?"

"I said, is everything okay back there?"

"Sure. Everything's just dandy."

"We'll stop a while."

"You don't have to do that on my account."

He stopped anyway. "You'll have to get off first so I can keep the bike steady."

She was no more graceful getting off than she had been getting on. Considering her train of thought for the last mile or so, that could turn into a very good thing. Obviously he'd brought her here to seduce her, cad that he was. C.J. longed for every unscrupulous thing he was fixing to do.

She'd even made up her mind to help him along. Why not? They were in a cow pasture surrounded by deep woods at least two miles from the nearest house. So what if she made a fool of herself? Nobody would see except the cows and one tired-looking old bull with a missing horn.

"This is the perfect place."

Clint cocked one eyebrow in that sexy move that nearly drove her crazy. He might as well have been crooking his finger at her. She slithered closer.

"The perfect place for what?"

"Whatever you have in mind." The coat she'd borrowed slid to the ground as she slunk closer in her borrowed dress.

He gave her a smoldering look that made her mouth go dry. "Princess, I believe you've read my mind."

"You tell me what's on your mind, and I'll tell you what's on mine."

"I prefer to show you."

He placed his mouth on hers before she could think. Oh, lord, what was happening to her? She'd never felt anything like this in her life.

Before today she thought she'd been kissed. She was mistaken. Clint's talented lips melted her bones, his marauding tongue stole her reason.

Heat consumed C.J., the heat of memories, the heat of the sun, the heat of hands. Clint's hands. Taking liberties with her.

C.J. wanted to scream, "Take me, take this cursed virginity. I want to feel like a real woman."

"You won't be needing this." His voice was thick with passion, his hand already on her zipper.

Oh help. When the dress parted he'd discover her padding.

"Wait."

"For what?"

Desperate, she cast about for a reason. "We haven't…we haven't seen the flowers."

"The what?"

"The wildflowers." On buttery legs she stumbled two feet away where the air wasn't so charged.

"You want to look at wildflowers?"

There was something dangerous in his voice. She didn't dare look at him.

"Yes. Smell that honeysuckle. Isn't it glorious?"
She took a deep steadying breath, still not daring to
glance his way.

"I hadn't noticed."

"Look at that black-eyed Susan." Her mind was
coming back, her vision was beginning to clear.
"There's some St. John's wort, and look over there
in the edge of the woods. Fire pink."

"My mother knew the names of all the wildflowers."

Something in his voice made her turn around. His
face was impassive, but Clint's eyes looked shattered.
C.J. was as shocked as if a wolf had turned into a lap
dog. He looked like a little boy who had suddenly
discovered he wouldn't have any Christmas this year.

C.J. wanted to reach out and smooth back his hair.
She wanted to gather him to her breasts and croon.
Considering recent events, that didn't seem wise.

"So does Dad. We used to walk together in the
evenings, and he'd point them out." He was very still,
watching her without really seeing. Where was he?
What was he remembering? "Did your mother teach
them to you?"

"It's getting late." He picked up her helmet and
tossed it to her. "Put this on."

"We're leaving?"

"Yes."

Saved, she thought. Relief flooded her as she
climbed on the motorcycle. Relief and regret. She'd
missed something important here.

Clint was furious at himself.

He was going soft. He'd had C. J. Maxey right in

the palm of his hand and had let her go...all because she knew the names of a few flowers. All because she widened those innocent-looking blue eyes of hers and acted like a shy, pure maiden.

He smacked his desk with his hand. He had to take his frustration out on something. Ever since he'd dropped her off at her car, he'd been a wild man. He'd nearly burned the keys off his computer typing up his story of the parade.

Shuffling through the piles of paper on his desk, he picked up pictures of C.J. You wouldn't know by looking that she was a hardhearted woman who could drive a man insane without even half trying.

He slammed the pictures on top of his story, threw the whole thing on Wayne's desk and jumped on his motorcycle. A few beers, that's what he needed. Something to cool him off and make him forget that C. J. Maxey was twisting him inside out and turning him upside down. Next thing you knew he'd be growing a conscience. Wouldn't that be a joke?

"I'll have your dress cleaned," C.J. said. She was next door, sitting in Sandi's kitchen sipping iced tea and eating tofu salad.

"Don't be silly. I didn't invite you over here to talk about the dress."

"What's up? You sounded so serious and mysterious on the phone."

"Oh, well, first tell me what you think of Clint Garrett."

"He's...interesting." C.J. didn't talk about relationships, even with her best friend. Not that she'd ever had one to talk about. She changed the subject. "So what is this news?"

"I'm thinking about getting married." Translated, that meant Sandi wanted a baby.

"That's not news."

Her friend wanted a family more than anybody C.J. had ever known. Sandi had been dreaming of starting her own family since she was sixteen, and probably would have ended up a teenage pregnancy statistic if Phoebe hadn't been there to guide her.

It seemed to C.J. that desire for family was no reason to marry, but who was she to judge? She knew nothing about the opposite sex and very little about romantic love except what she remembered of Sam and Phoebe before the accident.

"Look, I know my record with men isn't great," Sandi said. "But I think it's different this time. He's local for one thing."

"Is he the family type?"

"Hardly. But he has a great gene pool."

C.J. sighed. She hated seeing her friend disappointed time after time. "If you want a family, you'd better pick a family man."

"I think he can be persuaded."

There was no use trying to talk sense into Sandi. Besides, who was she to give advice about love?

"If anybody can do it, you can." C.J. lifted her glass. "Let's toast. Here's to success. May you get pregnant on your wedding night."

"If not sooner." Sandi clicked her glass against C.J.'s. "My biological alarm is going off."

Laughing, they drank their tea, then dug into their tofu salad.

"I'm glad he's local," C.J. said. "I'd hate to think of you moving off to Mexico or Tahiti. I'd miss this."

"Me, too."

"So who is he? Anybody I know?"

"Well, yes. I was going to tell you... It's Clint Garrett."

C.J. dropped her drink. Tea soaked her shorts and ran in rivulets down her legs. Glass shattered on the tile floor.

Sandi jumped up and swabbed C.J. with a dish towel. "Are you all right?"

"Of course I'm all right." She jerked the cloth away and angled herself so Sandi couldn't see her face. "It's only tea."

But it wasn't. It was a sexy man feeding her popcorn on the sofa. It was clinging to a set of broad shoulders while she whizzed through the countryside on his motorcycle. It was the kiss of a lifetime.

"You're sure? I would never dream of going after him if I thought for one minute that you were interested. I mean, he did escort *you* on the float."

"That's all he was. My escort." C.J. jumped up and stalked about the kitchen slamming cabinets. "Where's the broom?"

"In the laundry room. I'll get it."

"No, let *me*." C.J. had to keep moving or she would explode. In the laundry room she leaned her head against the wall and took a deep breath. But that didn't help a bit.

Sandi could have any man she wanted. Why did she want Clint? And why couldn't C.J. tell her, "No, I want him for myself?"

"Because it's ridiculous, that's why." Nobody in

Hot Coffee had ever looked at her twice. Why did she think a man like Clint Garrett would be interested? Certainly not on a permanent basis, not on a let's-have-a-baby basis.

There. She was as bad as Sandi. Longing for the impossible.

Of course, in Sandi's case, it wasn't impossible. She'd had a string of losers, that's all. Clint Garrett was no loser. He was just a little misguided, a little confused. Sandi would fix that with one dazzling smile.

C.J. would be her bridesmaid. She'd live next door to them and be godmother to their baby. She'd be gray before she'd forget the way Clint Garrett had kissed her, but she would keep her secrets.

Sandi was that rare and precious commodity, a true friend. C.J. wasn't about to jeopardize her friendship over a man who didn't even know she existed.

"C.J.?" Sandi was just outside the door, tapping. "Are you all right in there?"

"Yes, just getting the dustpan."

"I was just thinking. Why don't we drive over to Shady Grove tonight and go to that nice little bar that does karaoke?"

And chance running into Clint? She'd rather cover herself with peanut butter and hang out in a tree for the birds to peck.

"'Fraid I can't, Sandi. Dad was feeling kind of down after the parade. Memories of Mom, you know."

"Next time, then, I'll let you know how it all comes out."

"I can hardly wait."

C.J. hoped God had a sense of humor.

Chapter Five

Clint sat in a corner booth at Snookie's Den by himself nursing his second beer of the evening. This was just what he needed—a cold beer, a decent band playing, lots of good-looking women.

"Look but don't touch," he muttered. He'd had one close call today. He wasn't fixing to risk another. Not that there was much chance of it. He still couldn't get C.J. off his mind.

"Damn her sexy hide."

"I beg your pardon." The waitress jumped back.

"Not you." He tapped his glass. "One more of these, please."

"Sure thing, honey."

Even the way the waitress twitched her cute little butt didn't improve his mood. Maybe he should have invited Wayne. Or even Charlie. Not that Charlie could put two sentences together that didn't involve some kind of sport, but listening to the stats on Mississippi State's Bulldogs would have been better than flagellating himself over a princess who didn't even look like one. Shoot, she didn't act like one either. She didn't act like anybody Clint had ever known.

That was the only reason she fascinated him. Had to be. He was immune to women.

As he started his third beer he decided that maybe he'd take a look at what Snookie's Den had to offer after all. Maybe another woman was exactly what he needed. Hair of the dog, and all that.

"Hi." The knockout blonde standing beside his booth looked vaguely familiar, but the light was dim and he was well into his cups. "Do you mind if I join you?"

That dazzling smile. Now he remembered. "Sandi? Sandi Wentworth? Right?"

"Yes." She slid beside him and he smelled her perfume. Something subtly sexy. He liked that. He liked the way she was dressed, too. Simple jeans and a white shirt open at the neck showing a long slender throat and a hint of cleavage. When she bent over and nabbed some peanuts from the bowl, her hair shone in the lamplight. Altogether she was a dynamite package.

"I believe I saw you this afternoon," he said.

"Yes. I *love* parades and circuses. When I was eight I wanted to run away and be a trapeze artist."

She had the type of enthusiasm that should have been contagious. It did nothing for him except make him vaguely uncomfortable. And he knew exactly why.

He downed the rest of his drink in one gulp. He was going to ask Miss Sandi Wentworth to dance and forget all about a man-killer in a red dress.

Sandi leaned close. "The music's great. I love soft, slow ballads, don't you?"

Clint's heart rate shot up, his pulse did the fandango. The moment was right.

"Tell me about C.J.," he said.

All the lights were on and Ellie's VW bug was parked in the driveway. C.J. set out running, then burst through the front door out of breath.

"Dad! Ellie!"

Ellie stuck her head around the kitchen door. "In here, C.J."

Her hair poked out like porcupine quills from her habit of running her hands through it, and she was wearing an old shirt of Sam's, a blue-and-green plaid one C.J. had seen a dozen times out in the clinic. Pots and pans littered the kitchen counters and delicious smells wafted all over the house. Another of Ellie's habits: when she was upset she cooked.

"Where's Dad? Has anything happened? Is he all right?"

"Yes. He's okay. Here. Eat this." Ellie shoved a slice of lemon ice-box pie in her hand, then cut two for herself. "If I don't quit this comfort eating I'm going to be as big as my car."

C.J. could use a little comfort eating, herself. Even as she sat down and kicked off her shoes, Sandi was somewhere with Clint, probably already in his house, maybe even his bed.

She took an extra-big bite. "Let me guess. The parade brought back memories. Right?"

"You got it. I had a sneaking suspicion, so when I called the house and nobody answered I came right over. Found Sam sitting in the bedroom poring over albums of Phoebe in her beauty queen days. 'Look at her,' he said, 'is she not the most beautiful woman in the world,' and I told him she was, said she was the prettiest woman in Mississippi. Then he set in to talking about how he'd failed her, how he'd failed all of us."

Ellie's hands shook as she poured two cups of hot chocolate then squirted on the whipped cream. It brimmed over and puddled on the countertop. She sat down without even wiping it up, which told C.J. all she needed to know about Ellie's state of mind.

"You do too much for us, Ellie. Why don't you go home and rest?"

"For what? Sex?" Ellie slammed her cup down, then jumped up to cut herself a piece of chocolate cake. "The last sex I had was in 1977."

C.J. couldn't have been more shocked if Ellie had suddenly sprouted horns. "Well," she murmured, "I'm not sure…"

"I'm tired of being a reliable old maid. I'm sick of pretending I don't have a libido." She pounded her chest. "Underneath this flat chest beats the heart of a woman. A *real* woman."

"I know just how you feel."

"No, you don't. I'm *old*."

"Why, you're not…"

"I'm a dried-up old crone with an atrophied peach orchard." Ellie slammed her cup down so hard chocolate milk sloshed all over the table. "I ought to go in there and slap the tar out of him."

"Who?"

"Sam, that's who."

"Dad? You want to slap *Dad?*" Now C.J. was really alarmed. Had Ellie had a mild stroke? Gone crazy? Suffered a mental breakdown of some kind?

C.J. jumped up. "I'll call a doctor."

"I don't need a doctor." Ellie grabbed her car keys out of her purse. "What I need is a man."

She stalked out of the kitchen and slammed the back door so hard it echoed through the house. Roused from sleep, Sam padded down the hall wearing bedroom slippers and a fuzzy-headed look.

"Where's Ellie?" he asked.

"Gone."

"Gone? Where'd she go?"

C.J. kissed his cheek and said, "Go on back to bed, Dad. Everything's all right."

What was one more lie? Sam shuffled off and she gathered up pots and pans. She was probably the only available-and-looking-but-not-so-you-could-tell woman in Hot Coffee washing dirty dishes in the shank of a Saturday night.

Sam's snores echoed down the hall and grated along C.J.'s already ragged nerves. She turned on the radio to drown out the sounds, but they overrode the easy country ballad and reverberated through the kitchen.

C.J. couldn't stand her dull life a minute longer. She threw the dishcloth onto the countertop and said, "There, I'm throwing in the towel."

Then she marched down to her little girl's bedroom

and ripped the frilly lace curtains off the windows. A moon as big as Missouri beamed through her windows and fell across the stuffed animals on her spinster's bed. She grabbed the teddy bear by the arm and tossed him into the closet. Next went the pink elephant Sam had won for her at the county fair when she was six years old. With one sweep she scooped the rest of the menagerie into a sack and slammed the closet door on them.

As a declaration of womanhood, it wasn't much but C.J. felt a stirring inside herself. If it wasn't liberation, it was close enough.

She stripped down and then tossed her cotton undergarments into the garbage can. The next time she got a paycheck she was going to spend every bit of it on sexy underwear. Lacy thongs and bras, hose with seams up the back and garter belts made of satin and lace. Black. Everything black.

For now plain pink silk would have to do. Feeling reckless, she ditched the bra altogether. She wasn't Audrey Hepburn in the yellow sundress, but she wasn't dog meat either. She painted her lips, not bright red but just a touch of color, fluffed up her hair, then wrote a note to Sam.

> Dear Dad,
> I've gone to Shady Grove to catch up with Sandi. I'll probably spend the night with her. See you in the morning.
>
> Crystal Jean.

She didn't know why she signed the note that way except that her mother always said Crystal Jean was an important name that made people sit up and take notice.

C.J. doubted he would notice she was gone in the morning. And even if he did, he'd probably think she'd just gone to visit Ellie or Sandi.

Predictable and boring, that's what she was. To-night she was going to change that. If Sandi could go man-fishing in Shady Grove, so could she.

But not for Clint Garrett. Most certainly *not* for Clint. She wouldn't touch him with a twenty-nine-and-a-half foot pole.

She was looking for somebody nice. Somebody wearing a white shirt and tie and a smile that said *I'm friendly but not too dangerous.* Well, okay, it wouldn't hurt if this friendly stranger turned out to be a little bit on the wild side. Wearing cowboy boots, say. Or a touch of leather.

By the time C.J. got to Shady Grove she was sweat-ing. When she pulled into the parking lot at Snookie's Den and saw Clint's big Harley and Sandi's little car she nearly turned around and went home. They'd think she was spying, which she absolutely, positively was *not*.

Maybe she was curious a little, but that was all. Besides, didn't she have a right to go juking wherever she pleased?

C.J. got bravely out of her car and went inside.

Thank God they didn't see her. C.J. spotted a booth hidden in a dark corner.

"Take your order, hon?"

C.J. blindly viewed the list of exotic drinks. Beer she couldn't abide. Tasted like something that ought to be in a cup in the clinic's lab. Bourbon sounded too brave and strong.

"What's good?" she asked.

"How about something a little exotic?"

"Okay." If she leaned forward just a little bit she could see around the pole: she could watch Sandi and Clint without ever being spotted. Not that she was spying. Not by a long shot. She did notice, though, that they had their faces so close they could steal kisses if they wanted to. She watched to see if they would, but they just kept talking and talking.

"Hon?"

C.J. stabbed randomly at the drink menu. "I'll take this one."

"Be right back."

It wasn't until the waitress had gone that C.J. saw what she'd selected—a green monkey. Nature's color. Cute little animal. It sounded harmless enough.

Clint was enjoying Sandi's latest C.J. tale, the one where they'd climbed a fig tree in order to escape the deadly pig trotting toward them in the pigsty.

"I don't know how we ended up in the pigsty in the first place, except that C.J. was always challenging me to do something Phoebe had forbidden, usually something that involved getting dirty and getting into trouble."

Her mother, the beauty queen. Clint could picture it, a defiant little girl who would think herself homely no matter how she looked, and all because her mother was renowned for her looks and charm.

"I think she was trying hard to be just like her father," Sandi added.

Clint didn't challenge her, but he had an entirely different picture of C.J. as a child. She'd been a little girl who desperately wanted to be like her mother, but because she thought she never could she did everything in her power to prove herself unworthy.

"Anyhow," Sandi continued, "as we clambered to safety the limb broke and we both ended up in the mud with the pig breathing down our necks. I screamed, but do you know what C.J. did?"

"Something bold."

"Exactly. When that old sow started rooting around in the mud, C.J. jumped on her back and yelled, 'Ride 'em, cowboy.'"

They lapsed into a friendly and comfortable silence while the band played an old Hank Williams song that made Clint think about dancing close with a woman's head on his shoulder and the smell of her perfume filling him up with sweet sadness.

Sandi glanced at her watch. "It's getting late."

"We never did dance," he said.

"That's okay." He took the slender hand she held out. "Thank you for not letting me make a fool of myself."

"Thank *you*." He leaned over and kissed her cheek. "Are you sure you won't let me see you home?"

"Positive. I've been taking care of myself for a very long time."

There was no self-pity in her tone, but underneath that smile was a bone-deep sadness he knew and understood, one that wouldn't go away. He might as well go home.

"I'll walk you to your car."

* * *

The green monkey was neither cute nor benign, but it was too late to do anything about that now because Clint and Sandi were coming her way. C.J. ducked behind her pole, but not before she'd seen how they kissed. Actually he'd done the kissing and only on her cheek that C.J. knew of. She'd probably missed the best ones, the one with lips locked and tongues entangled.

Look at the bright side, though, they'd probably name their first child after her. Girl or boy, it wouldn't matter.

"C.J.?" C.J. jumped a mile, and when she landed back in her seat she saw that Sandi and Clint had launched a sneak attack.

"What are you doing here?" Sandi's smile looked the same, but C.J. wasn't fooled. She'd been misplaced by Clint Garrett. Or was that *dis*placed?

Oh, she couldn't think. Green monkeys were stomping around her head and making all sorts of diversionary noises.

"I'm uh...drinking mean gunkeys." A big hiccup exploded, and from the way they were looking at C.J. you'd think she was the one who had done it. Well, she knew good and well she hadn't because that wasn't nice manners, and if there was one thing she had it was nice manners.

"She never has had a head for alcohol," Sandi told Clint, and C.J. stood up to defend herself.

But the floor was warped and it tossed her back onto her seat in an undignified heap.

When Sandi said, "I'd better take her home," C.J. noticed that at a certain angle her neck looked long and not at all graceful but more like something you'd want to hide under turtleneck sweaters. She was on the verge of pointing that out when she remembered the red sequined dress, and so she forgave Sandi's fatal flaw because of her past generosity.

"I'm not going," she said.

Sandi leaned close, and of course C.J. saw that she was mistaken. Her friend had a graceful neck and furthermore there was not a single flaw in her face or her figure, which made C.J. wish for another of those monkey drinks. Purple this time, because obviously green was the color of envy and that's why her brain felt warped and she felt surly.

"But, C.J....."

"You go on with Mishter Gilded."

Clint took Sandi's arm. "Come on, I'll see you to your car then..." His words got lost as he hightailed it out of there, which just proved how eager he was to help out a woman with an exploding biological clock.

C.J. tortured herself thinking about the two of them in a tangle of love, then she braved the undulating sea of pea-green carpet in order to find the bathroom.

Her caged monkeys were looking for escape.

Chapter Six

When he discovered C.J. missing from her booth Clint mentally kicked himself for going off and leaving her in that condition in the first place. He felt a tightening in his chest like a man about to have a heart attack.

He hadn't felt this anxious since he'd played hooky from eighth grade then had to face the disappointment of his mother.

It served him right. He knew better than to embrace chivalry and honor.

If he weren't careful he'd discover he had a heart. Even worse, others would discover it. Sandi probably already had. All that big talk about getting information on C.J. for his articles… He'd be willing to bet his Harley that she'd seen right through him.

Tomorrow he'd do some damage control. He'd find a party girl and flaunt her all around town.

Clint sighed. He wasn't going to do that. He was going to find C.J. and rescue her, and for no other reason than the insistent demands of his newly awakened conscience.

The woman who had waited his table was Gloria. "Have you seen the woman in yellow who was sitting in that corner booth?"

"Yes. She went into the ladies' room about ten minutes ago."

A lot of things could happen in ten minutes, every one of them bad. Clint imagined each one in vivid detail... C.J. passed out on a stone-cold floor, her head gashed open from her fall. C.J. too sick to stand, clinging to the edge of the toilet and moaning his name. C.J. abducted. The most sensational crime Hot Coffee had ever seen.

"Would you mind going in there and seeing about her? She's not in very good condition."

"Sure. Be right back."

"And, Gloria, don't mention that I sent you."

It couldn't have been more than three minutes until Gloria emerged from the ladies' room with C.J. in tow, but in that time Clint aged ten years.

"You scared me to death." He scooped up C.J. and held her close, and darned if he didn't feel like some kind of hero in a Greek myth.

"Wha'?"

"I'm taking you home."

It was only after he got to the parking lot that he realized his dilemma. Obviously he couldn't haul her off on the back of his bike because she was in no condition to hang on.

He propped C.J. against the wall and rummaged

through her purse looking for car keys. He'd never seen as much stuff in his life—six-months-old receipts, scraps of paper with snippets written down in some undecipherable code, a thousand tubes of lip balm, fourteen pens, earrings without their backings. What did women do? Keep their filing and book-keeping in their purses? Use them as garbage cans?

Why couldn't women be more like men? That's what he wanted to know.

Thankfully C.J. was quiet during his long quest for keys. When he found them he hauled her over his shoulder and folded her into the front seat of her car. Her eyes looked so glazed he checked her pulse. Still beating.

Though he was not responsible for her condition, there was no way he could take her back to Sam, though God knows what he was going to do with her when he got her home. She roused briefly when he turned into his apartment complex.

"This is not my housh."

"I know."

"Where Shandi?"

"She left before we did."

He parked in the garage where he usually kept his Harley, and when he lifted her out of the car she lolled in his arms and gave him a stern look.

"Unhand me, shir."

"No way. Think of this as a pajama party, just the two of us."

"Don't like pajamas."

"That's okay. You can sleep in the nude."

"With you?"

The sheer artlessness of the question caught him

off guard. Lord, how was he ever going to get through the night without losing his sanity and his honor?

The first battle hadn't even started, but with her sweet weight in his arms he was already losing the war. Best thing he could do was get off the battle-ground.

He tossed her over his shoulder so he could fit the key into the lock. His bedroom lay straight ahead. All he had to do was deposit her on the bed and shut the door, then he'd be home free. But first he had to make it to the door. First he had to traverse a huge expanse of living room that looked as hot and endless as the Mojave.

"Here goes," he said, and C.J. giggled.

Suddenly the green monkeys made it all so clear to her: she was desirable, she was invincible and she was getting a second chance to have a taste of excess. No, not just a taste. A huge dose.

"Here goesh wha'?"

"Torture."

She'd had something else in mind, but if he was into kinky stuff she'd try to play that game provided it could be done upside down. Dangling over his shoulder she latched on to the first delicious-looking target she saw. His jeans were tight, his back pocket was handy and his backside was sooo enticing. She slid her hand inside and began to massage.

"What are you doing?" He pulled back so hard she lost her breath.

"Foreplay."

"What?"

"I said FOREPLAY. Have you lost your min'?"

"No. Only my sanity."

That struck her as funny, and she had to recover from another fit of giggles before she could continue her erotic games. She hiccupped once which put her face in the vicinity of his neck, his thick, muscular, manly smelling neck that was too good to resist. She took a little nip, and when he yelped she licked it to make it all better.

"Would you stop that?"

"You don' like it?"

"That's not the problem."

"Problem?"

"I like it too much."

That sounded good to C.J. Better than good. It sounded like encouragement, so she looked around for another place to lick. His ear was right there, pink- ish and curved just right for her tongue. She plunged right in and he made groaning sounds which could have been good or bad. Being new at all this, she couldn't tell.

"Like it?" she whispered, and when he didn't an- swer she took his silence for consent and did it all over again.

She was turning out to be a natural. Why hadn't anybody told her? Why had she waited till she was practically over the hill before she'd found her true self?

Wouldn't her ex-friend Sandi turn green with envy?

With a sound like an aroused bull elephant, Clint charged toward the bedroom, kicked open the door and dumped her onto the bed. There was only so much torture a man could endure.

"You want to play games, do you?"

"What kind?"

"Don't widen those blue eyes at me, princess. You know exactly what kind."

Silencing the voice of his newfound conscience, Clint jerked off his shirt. Buttons flew every which way, and damned if the little minx in his bed didn't grab a handful of bedcovers and pretend to cower in terror.

"Your little act won't wash with me. You've been asking for this ever since I brought you home."

She hiccupped once, then covered her mouth with her hand. "S'cuse me."

"If you think you can change things with a latent attack of manners, you're wrong."

He flung his constricting jeans to the floor and stalked toward the bed. The mattress sank under the weight of his knee, and she scuttled to the far side of the bed. He grabbed her foot and hauled her toward him.

"Bravo, C.J. You could go onstage with that modest act."

"It's not an act."

"Are you telling me the woman who licked my neck like an expert courtesan is scared?"

Her eyes shot daggers as she jerked out of his reach. "There's nothing I enjoy more than a fiery woman." He snaked out one arm and dragged her back. She went as stiff and scratchy as an overstarched shirt. "Make no mistake about it, princess. I plan to enjoy you to the hilt."

"With that golden sword of yoursh?"

"You do have a way with words." He tightened his hold and discovered she wasn't wearing a bra. The thin fabric of her summer sundress only heightened his excitement. "Let's see how you are with actions."

He claimed her sweet open mouth then lingered there for such a long time he remembered such things as innocence and tenderness.

C.J. made a little moaning sound, and he tore himself away from her intoxicating lips.

"Hmm," she murmured. "I like that."

Amazing, her ability to keep throwing him curves. "You do?"

"Yes. I've never been kissed like that."

His wicked intentions fled like a flock of naughty children.

"You are the damnedest woman I've ever met."

"And you are the dam'dish man."

"You're also very drunk."

"Am not."

"Are, too." He had to laugh. Just look at him, sitting on his own bed with a ready woman in his arms, and all he could think about was how he was going to get her out of her dress and into a pair of his pajamas without shocking her modesty.

She tilted her head back and looked at him with pouty lips. "Kiss me again."

"Not tonight, princess."

"Why not?"

"Because I make it a habit never to take advantage of an inebriated woman. The problem with you is, I keep forgetting."

"Caush o' me?"

"Yes, because of you."

She gave him an arch smile. "Am I shexy?"

"You are very *shexy*."

She giggled and that started a gale of hiccups. He pounded her on the back, and when that didn't work he kissed her again. It was the only thing to do.

She melted against him, making little moaning sounds of pleasure, and what could he do but lower her to the mattress and mold her against his near-naked body? After all, he was only human.

And she was only a natural. Her hands knew exactly what to do, exactly which spots to touch. His arousal was immediate and insistent.

The devil in him said, Go on, do it. She wants it. All you have to do is lift her skirt and slide down her panties. But the aggravating angel over his shoulder said, Even you draw the line at this.

Clint broke off the kiss and sat up, taking her with him.

"Upsy daisy."

"Wha?"

"Bedtime, princess."

"With you?"

"No. Tonight we sleep in separate beds."

She looked so forlorn he had to stifle his laughter.

"It'sh 'cause of the panties."

"What?"

"They're pink."

"Are you describing your underwear to me, Miss Maxey?"

"You wanna see?"

He grabbed her hands before she could lift her skirt. "Not tonight. I'm in no condition to withstand further goading."

She pouted at him. "They're tacky."

He suppressed another laugh. "Back to the panties, are we?"

"Not bikinis."

"No?"

"They're granny britches. Cover the subject."

"I see." He hadn't been this entertained since he'd interviewed her through the bathroom door. If it weren't for his rather painful state, he'd be enjoying the hell out of himself. "And which subject would that be?"

"The peach orchard."

"The what?"

"Tha's wha' Ellie calls it."

She giggled and he couldn't work up more than a grin because he was having the devil of a time with images of peaches—lush, ripe and juicy.

"You love Ellie, don't you?"

"Yes. She's been a mother."

"Then she'll thank me for what I'm about to do." He got up off the bed and jerked his pants on. "I'm going to get you a pair of my pajamas so you won't have to sleep in your pretty yellow dress."

She didn't say anything which was probably a good thing, because the way she looked lying on his bed was more than enough to make walking out of the room one of the hardest things he'd ever done.

"Be right back," he said, then hurried out before he tossed his worrisome conscience out the window and fell upon that fallen yellow flower.

He stubbed his toe in the dark and said an evil word, but it didn't ease his state of mind one bit. Just thinking about what he'd left behind was enough to arouse a sleeping giant. He jerked open a drawer and nabbed a pair of green silk pajamas, a gift from a misguided mistress whose name he couldn't even remember.

He stubbed the same toe in the same dark, but refrained from any more profanity just in case C.J. had fallen asleep and he could leave the pajamas draped on the end of the bed where she would see them if she woke up.

No such luck. She'd heard him coming. Before he even got to the door she said, "You don't have to tiptoe. We're all alone."

When he rounded the door frame, he lost what shred of control he'd managed to find. C.J. was standing in the middle of the room with her dress pooled at her feet, her pert little breasts calling his name and her trim little bottom encased in a pair of pink silk panties that screamed innocence but whispered erotica.

"The zipper was hard."

"That's not the only thing."

"I wanted you to unzip me, but you left."

Her pouty mouth beckoned, but he knew if he kissed her now he'd never stop.

"I see you managed fine without me."

He'd never seen anything more desirable than her lips. Except her breasts. He wanted to devour them, to take her taut pink nipples deep into his mouth and feast an hour or two.

"If it's any consolation, princess, I want you, too. Unfortunately I've discovered a troublesome streak of nobility."

She put her hands on her hips, which caused the

rest of her to move in a most enticing way. "Drat," she said.

"Those aren't exactly my sentiments, but they'll do." He tossed the pajamas onto the end of the bed. "Put these on."

"Don't want to."

"Whatever you wish. They're yours if you need them. Good night, princess."

"Wait. Where'you goin'?"

"To bed."

Her face lit up. "With me?"

"Not tonight. When I go to bed with you, you'll be in a condition to remember every single detail."

Her luscious pink mouth fell open, but he didn't stay to find out whether she wanted to speak or merely to be kissed. He did what any sane red-blooded male would do under the circumstances: he fled.

Chapter Seven

Ordinarily Clint fell into bed and didn't move till morning. It was one of his greatest achievements, being able to sleep the sleep of the innocent in spite of his wicked ways. But tonight storm troopers in hobnailed boots marched through his head and every one of them shouted her name.

He untangled himself from the covers that wrapped around him like a boa constrictor. He was already out the door when he remembered he wasn't wearing a stitch, so he raced back to the bed and wrapped the sheet around himself. He was glad nobody could see him—a grown man who ought to know better, tiptoeing around in his own house wearing the bedcovers.

"This damned nobility is killing me."

In spite of that, he pressed on. Just to make sure C.J. wasn't asleep on the floor or lying in the bathroom with her head cracked open. She was in such a state that any number of dire things could have happened to her.

Not that it mattered to him one way or the other. In spite of the way she kissed. In spite of the way he desired her. He just wanted to get her back to Sam Maxey's in one piece, that's all.

She'd fallen asleep with the light on. For a moment Clint stood in the doorway merely looking at her, feasting his eyes like a man too long deprived of the company of women, which was about the most ridiculous thing he could think of. If Wayne could see him now he'd say Clint had lost his marbles. He'd suggest his ace reporter take a long vacation in a secure place with bars on the windows and nurses in soft-soled shoes.

What he ought to do was turn around and leave Hot Coffee's most exasperating woman on top of the covers. He was used to taking the easy way out, so why not just turn around and walk back down the hall and get on with the battle of the bedsheets?

Sighing, he picked up the silk pajamas she'd kicked onto the floor then knelt beside the bed and took one slender foot in his hand. It *was* cold. She was liable to get sick if he didn't do something.

And so he made the supreme sacrifice. He sat on the edge of the bed and shifted her legs into his lap.

C.J. stirred, Clint bit back a groan then eased her legs into the pajamas. He took his time, too. Not that he wanted to feel her silky skin. He didn't want to wake her. That was all.

Not that there was much chance of that. She lay across his lap like a felled sapling. The only difference was, he'd never had a burning desire to run his hands over a felled sapling. Lord, she was enticing lying there with his pajamas gathered around her tiny waist and her beautiful bare torso screaming for his attention.

He had to compose himself before he could even pick up the pajama top. Getting her into it was going to take some finesse…and all the control he could muster.

Taking a deep breath he gingerly lifted her left arm…and all hell broke loose.

She screeched like a banshee then reared up and whacked his chin with a fist.

"What are you doing?" he asked.

It seemed a reasonable question to him, but C.J. took umbrage. Her fist smashed him again, this time in the eye.

"Dammit," he roared. "Stop that."

He tried to grab her wrists but she rolled sideways, then kicked him with the feet he'd so recently admired. He was rapidly revising his opinion. Those formerly dainty feet packed a punch like a peenball hammer.

To make matters worse he could hardly see out of the eye she'd smacked, plus he was having trouble fending her off and hanging on to his bedsheet. How could he hold on to his makeshift toga and fend off flailing arms and legs and flying fists?

He let go of her arm long enough to grab a corner of the sheet, and she landed a blow to his other eye.

That was the last straw. The only way to win this war was to fight dirty.

"You'd better batten down the hatches, princess, because I've had enough."

She was going to pulverize the two-timing alley cat. In one day he'd tried to seduce her in a cow pasture, carried her former best friend off for nefarious purposes, then lured C.J. to his bed. Never mind that she couldn't hold her liquor. All the more reason for him to act the gentleman.

Clint grabbed for her and she ducked, which turned out to be most unfortunate because it put her face in such close proximity to his most enthralling body parts that she almost hyperventilated.

C.J. was going to thank Sandi for rescuing her…if she could ever forgive her for taking him away. She readjusted her focus to a less unsettling view—Clint's amused face.

Her curtsey proved another major mistake in a day fraught with them. She jerked upright with a flaming face and the fervent hope that he hadn't noticed the direction of her gaze.

Not only did his diabolical laughter confirm her fears, but his wicked gaze burned her to a cinder. "Keep doing that and we'll both be in trouble, princess."

"Stop ogling me."

"You shouldn't prance around half naked if you don't want your considerable assets to be appreciated."

"I'm not prancing…I'm running, you fool."

"No need. I've stopped chasing you, or have you been too busy to notice?"

She stormed away and covered herself with the first

thing she could find. Wouldn't you know it would smell exactly like him, good clean soap and a subtle, spicy aftershave with just a hint of musky male sweat.

C.J. clutched the sheet close around her neck, then held it out tent-style so he couldn't see what the heady combination of aromas was doing to her traitorous breasts. She felt like one of those women who had been kidnapped by scoundrels and been brainwashed until she was just like her captors. Maybe there was a good book she could read in order to deprogram herself.

He leaned against the chest of drawers, obviously enjoying her discomfort. "Do you think you can hide from me behind that sheet?"

She flushed so hot she felt as if she'd fallen into a bed of fire ants.

"It will take a bigger man than you to get me out."

The minute the words were out of her mouth, she wanted to take them back, but it was far too late. Suddenly, the debonair man at the door had vanished and in his place stood a man with fire in his eyes and thunder in his soul.

"The next time you go on a quest for a worthy man, Miss Maxey, I suggest you look somewhere besides Snookie's Den." He stalked toward the door, then turned back to her. "Rest well for what's left of the night. In the morning you're going to need it."

She vaguely remembered that they'd come back to his apartment in her car. If only she could remember where she'd put the keys.

As if he'd read her mind, he said, "Don't bother looking for the keys. I've got them somewhere safe." His smile would frost hot biscuits. "Sleep tight, princess."

Chapter Eight

Around five o'clock Clint gave up his battle for sleep and sanity. He slipped into his clothes, dashed off a note then sneaked into the camp of the enemy. She lay on her left side with her legs curled and her cheek resting on her folded hands. Danger masquerading as a lamb. Poison posing as innocence.

The sooner he got out of there the better off he was. Tiptoeing like a thief in his own house, he cast the note onto the bedside table and made his escape.

A taxi was waiting outside to take him into Shady Grove for his motorcycle. He had no travel plan and no destination. The point was simply leaving. Who knows, maybe he'd find a town somewhere with a good mom-and-pop restaurant that served grilled hamburgers as big as flying saucers and a secluded fishing hole where a man could sit on the poolbank, drop a line in the water and not think about anything except how long it would be before the fish started biting. A welcoming kind of place where he could hang his hat for a little while.

Clint jumped on his bike and headed east toward Alabama.

C.J. had made a royal mess of things. Her fury at Clint had not abated, but mostly she was furious with herself. Sitting in the middle of her own bed in her crumpled hair shirt, formerly known as a yellow sundress, she read the two notes for the dozenth time.

"C.J.," her dad had written, "I've gone to church, back around noon, hope you had a good time with Sandi."

Guilt pangs squeezed her deceitful heart, and she crumpled her dad's note and tossed it into the wastebasket.

Clint's was equally brief, equally guilt-producing. "Princess," it read, "here are your car keys. Hope you find your worthy man. Happy hunting."

This one she didn't toss aside, but instead put it under her pillow where it would be a constant reminder that women who pretend to be somebody they're not deserve exactly what they get. The problem was not that she had agreed to be Lee County's Dairy Princess, but that she had presented herself as a whole 'nother person, which had set up expectations for things she couldn't deliver. Not only that, but her posturing had cost her a best friend, caused Ellie pain, and driven a wedge between her and her dad. In addition, she had willfully hurt another human being.

Maybe Clint Garrett wasn't the world's most desirable bachelor, but he didn't deserve to feel unworthy as a toad.

C.J. had some bridges to repair, and she was going to start with Ellie.

She lived in a small white house near the post office, protected from the spying eye of the postmistress by a thick row of gardenias, an arbor heavy with pink-and-white roses, and countless flowerbeds filled with iris and lilies, phlox and lavender, azalea and forsythia already gone by. Fragrant culinary herbs in pots perfumed the walkway and verbena laid a carpet of purple around an ancient bird bath where two fat robins were taking a break from feeding the babies that nested in the hanging ferns on the front porch.

Ellie's straw hat bobbed among the riot of blossoms in the English garden she'd created from scratch.

"Yahoo," she called when she spotted C.J. Discarding her gloves and her gardening shears, she nodded toward the porch swing. "Have a seat and tell me what's wrong."

"I don't want to interrupt your gardening."

"Interrupt it. I'm just out here puttering around so I wouldn't have to go to church and face Sam."

Right then and there C.J. decided that for once she wasn't going to be the one spilling problems for Ellie to fix.

"I'm worried about you, Ellie."

"No need. I'm a tough old nut. I can survive anything."

"I shouldn't have let you leave the house in the state you were in last night."

"Don't worry about me, C.J. I called Lucy, and

she and Kitty and Dolly came over with elderberry wine. The Foxes always pull each other through.''

Phi Omicron Xi, nicknamed the Foxes. The sorority Ellie and her three friends had chartered in rebellion against the snobbish social clubs they'd encountered on campus. Phoebe had told her the story a dozen times, how the four smartest women on campus had asked her to join them even though she couldn't hold a candle to them intellectually. ''I guess they must have felt sorry for me, because I was something of an outsider myself,'' Phoebe would say. ''Nobody could get beyond my beauty titles till the Foxes came along.''

Ellie had told a different story: ''Phoebe was the lightning rod that kept us grounded. The rest of us would have vanished into a cosmic fog if it hadn't been for your mother.''

Phoebe had played the same role in their family, and when she died Sam *had* vanished, only returning in brief spurts, mostly when Ellie was around.

''Tell me what happened between you and Dad last night.''

''Nothing.''

One thing C.J. had learned from watching her dad at the clinic was patience. She sat back on the cushions and waited for Ellie to tell her the truth.

''Don't look at me like that, C.J.''

''Like what?''

''Like Sam. He has a way of tilting his head and pulling the truth out of you with his eyes.''

That's when it hit C.J. that Ellie was more than a good friend to her family, more than a surrogate mother to her.

"How long have you been in love with my father?"

"How did you know?"

"I guess I finally grew up."

"Do you want some tea?"

"No, thank you, Ellie. But I do want to know about you and Dad."

"We grew up together."

"I already know that. Tell me something I don't know, like when you fell in love with him and why he married my mother instead of you."

"Good lord, anybody in his right mind would choose Phoebe over me. Your mother was not only beautiful, she was charming and sweet. Everybody loved her. Sam was smitten from the moment he met her."

Which had been when they were in college.

"What I want to know is *before* college. I want to know about you and Dad."

Ellie smiled at her. "You're just like Sam. You won't be satisfied till you get to the bottom of all this."

"I love both of you, Ellie, and I don't like to see you as unhappy as you were last night."

"What about Sam? He's been unhappy for six years."

"I wish I knew what to do about that."

"Why don't you try not to coddle him? Why don't you try living your life, no matter where it takes you?"

"And leave Dad behind?"

"Yes." Ellie gazed over the porch railing at her

roses as if she were taking strength from their beauty. "Maybe it's time we both quit trying to protect him."

C.J. thought Ellie might be right, but she wasn't ready to admit any drastic changes into her life. First she had to get her feet planted solidly back on the ground and then she had to repair fences.

"Were you and Dad ever planning to marry?"

"Yes. I've loved Sam forever, I guess. From the time we played in the same sandbox to the time we partnered on the debate team in high school, we were a couple. Everybody took for granted that someday we'd marry. I wanted it with my whole heart, and I guess he just went along with it, being Sam."

"I doubt that. Dad rarely does a thing simply because that's what everybody expects. In fact, just the opposite is true. I think he sometimes does the unexpected just to prove what a maverick he is. Or he *used* to."

"You really think so?"

"I *know* so."

"Well, whatever he felt for me couldn't hold firm in the face of Phoebe's charms." Ellie sighed. "I was the one he escorted to the dance that night. Phoebe was the one he took home."

It amazed C.J. how her situation paralleled Ellie's. Like her old friend before her, she couldn't hold a candle to Sandi's beauty and charm. Who could blame Clint Garrett for falling at Sandi's feet?

Apparently history was going to repeat itself: she would play Ellie's role, the maiden lady who hovered on the sidelines with a heart full of unrequited love.

"How did you and Mom manage to remain friends after that? Didn't you feel betrayed?"

"Yes, for a while. By both of them. I guess Phoebe and I didn't speak for months, and then I got to missing her. She was always the one cracking jokes and thinking up fun things to do. Without her, my life was drab and boring, and so I locked up my feelings for Sam and forgave Phoebe."

"And never found anybody else…"

"I didn't even try."

"Do you regret that?"

"My life is what it is. I accept things as they are and try not to have regrets."

"I wish I could be like that. Ellie, I have something to confess to you."

"You hate being the dairy princess."

"How did you know?"

"My dear, anybody who loves you can see that. And I love you as if you were my own."

"I love you, too, Ellie. You've been a mother to me."

"I'm sorry I ever got you into it. You can give up your title if you want to. No harm done."

"I'm no quitter."

"I know that, still I don't want you to be miserable in a role that makes you uncomfortable."

"What if I just be myself? What if I forget about the padded bras and the excess makeup and the posturing and just act naturally?"

"Honey, that's all I ever wanted you to be in the first place."

C.J. laughed. "Why didn't you say so? Then I wouldn't have sweated all over Sandi's red dress."

"I thought you wanted to make yourself over."

"Not anymore. I can probably kiss any chance of

winning a scholarship goodbye, but no more slinky red dresses for me. I promise you this, though, I'm going to be the best plain princess the dairy industry ever had. I want you to be proud of me.''

"I *am* proud of you. Who knows how it will all turn out? I think the tide in these pageants is turning in favor of smart sensible girls.''

After the events of the past few days C.J. had a hard time thinking of herself as either smart or sensible. But there was one thing she knew for sure, she wasn't going to sit around and wait for turning tides to determine her fate. She wasn't fixing to end up in a cottage all by herself with nothing to look forward to except deadheading roses and an occasional afternoon on the back porch sipping tea with a man who didn't know she was in the world.

The sign said Reform. Clint didn't miss the irony. Although he had no intention of taking its advice he did take the sign as an omen and stopped at a small café on the outskirts of the small Alabama town.

He needed an oversized cup of coffee, a big mess of collards and cornbread and a telephone, in that order. The waitress came to the table bearing a coffee urn, which was one of the things Clint loved about the South. No messing around on formalities. Just nod your head, flip your cup upright and wait for your first fortifying drink.

"Cream and sugar?" The waitress's name tag said Lorraine.

"No thanks, Lorraine." The first drink jolted him all the way to his toes, and he gave the waitress a smile of pure satisfaction. That's all it took to make them bosom buddies.

"It'll put hair on your chest, hon."

"Just what I need."

"Pshaw. You look like the kind of man just full of piss and vinegar."

He'd thought so, too, till he tangled with a crazy-making woman named Crystal Jean Maxey.

"I'm about a quart low."

"Well, hon, we'll try to fix you right up. What can I get for you today?"

He spied just what he wanted on the menu, and when he ordered, Lorraine said, "You've hit the jack-pot. It comes with the best chicken and dumplings in Alabama." She winked. "I'll make sure you get the best parts of the chicken."

True to her word, she heaped his plate with enough food to sustain two grown men plus a hound dog under the table.

"Do you serve food like this every day?"

"Every day except Sunday, and Mike says—that's my sweet husband, we own this place—if the Almighty had to take a day off to rest, I guess the good folks of Reform can wait for me to do the same thing."

She pronounced the name with a heavy accent on the first syllable, and Clint decided then and there that he could live in a town like that, a town where the café owner's wife made sure a man had food that would stick to his bones and plenty of coffee to keep him warm on a cold winter's night...or in this case, bring him back to life on a hot summer's day.

"What's the matter, hon? Ghosts walking on your grave?"

Clint was losing his grip. Once, he could win six hands straight and then use the same poker face to tell a lie that would gain him entry into a sweet-faced woman's warm bed.

Now look at him. He couldn't get in a woman's bed on a bet, and waitresses in Reform, Alabama, were ready to send him sympathy cards.

Of course, C.J. wasn't just any woman. And there had been his woeful attack of honor.

"No." Another lie, hopefully with a face not so bald. "If you've got some good fishing holes, I might just pack up and move here."

"My husband Mike's the best fisherman in Reform. He'd show you a few." She poured him a fresh cup of coffee without even asking. "And, hon, if you need anything, finding a place to work or anything, just come here and talk to Mike. He's a pure miracle worker, that man of mine."

"Thanks for the offer."

Clint left Lorraine an outrageously generous tip, then went outside to the free-standing pay phone in the parking lot. He put in his change and dialed his editor.

"What're you doing, Wayne?"

"I was napping till somebody who ought to know better than to call a working man on a hot Sunday afternoon got me up off the couch. This had better be good."

"I'm moving."

"This is supposed to be news? You said that last year."

"Yeah, but this time I mean it."

"Finally decided to take my advice and move to Atlanta where you could put your talent to use, did you?"

"No. I've decided to move to Reform."

"Reform, *Alabama?*"

"That's right. They make the best chicken and dumplings in the South, and they've got people here you could cotton to if you took a notion."

"Cut the bull. What's going on...and don't tell me it's chicken and dumplings?"

It was on the tip of his tongue to say *C.J.,* but Clint knew he'd sorely regret his slip of the tongue tomorrow.

"It's time to move on, that's all."

He could feel Wayne's roaring silence all the way across the state line. The sun beat down on Clint's head, scorching his brains and he wished two things—that he hadn't left his cell phone on his hall table and that he hadn't left his helmet hanging on the handle bars of his Harley.

Three things, actually. He wished he'd never laid eyes on a woman named Crystal Jean Maxey.

Finally Wayne broke his brooding silence. "I suspect you wouldn't be waking me up to tell me this on a Sunday afternoon when you could have told me the same thing in the morning unless you're dead-dog serious and fixing to make a break for it right now."

"You got it."

"You think it's that easy, huh? Just pick up and walk out?"

"I'm giving you notice."

"I'm not accepting it. I've got a newspaper con-

vention in Biloxi to go to and I sure as hell can't go
and leave Charlie in charge.''

''When's the convention?''

''The last of July.''

''Shoot, Wayne, that's a month away.''

''One more month in Hot Coffee's not going to kill
you.''

It just might. But he couldn't tell that to Wayne
either.

''All right. A month, but that's it. Then I'm leaving.''

Chapter Nine

"The phone's ringing, C.J."

Sam appeared in his bathrobe, although it was two in the afternoon, to impart this information to C.J. as if she weren't perfectly capable of hearing the telephone.

"Can you answer it, Dad?"

"It's not likely to be for me."

"Still, I'm busy here." She held up a fat book of statistics about the dairy industry in Mississippi.

"Well, all right. I guess I can get it."

He walked like a very old man when he left the room.

"Dad, if it's Sandi, tell her I'm busy."

"C.J., I don't understand this. That's what I told her yesterday and the day before."

"I know, but will you please tell her again?"

By the time they'd finished waltzing around this topic, the phone had stopped ringing. C.J. felt reprieved, though knew it wouldn't last long. Sandi wasn't the type to give up, and C.J. knew she couldn't keep avoiding her. Eventually the truth would have to come out.

"I guess whoever it was will call back." Sam eased into his recliner then picked up his newspaper and turned on the lamp although it was broad daylight and he didn't need it to see. This little ritual took several minutes, then he polished his glasses, put them on, took them off and polished them again in another of the small daily routines that ate away time and fooled him into thinking his life was busy and full.

C.J. had never recognized it for what it was, but now she saw the narrowness of Sam's life…and hers. Ellie was right. It was time to move on. If she didn't she'd end up just like her father, petrified, habits and thoughts solidified into a pattern as rigid and unyielding as the statue of the Confederate soldier that stood in the town square over in Shady Grove.

Looking over the tops of his glasses, he cleared his throat, which meant he had something important to say. It was just another little quirk, but today it irritated C.J.

"Have you seen Ellie lately?" he asked.

"Not since Sunday. Have you?"

"No. I wonder why she hasn't dropped by."

"Maybe she's waiting for an invitation."

"Ellie doesn't need an invitation. She's part of the family."

"Not really, Dad."

"I thought you loved her."

"I do. And she loves us. Especially you."

Sam picked up his paper, shook it out, held it in front of his face as if he were suddenly absorbed, then folded it twice and laid it back down.

"What do you mean by that?" he said.

"Just what I said. Why don't you call her?"

"She's probably busy."

"Call her and find out."

"She'll drop by in a few days."

"I wouldn't count on it."

"She's been doing it for years. I don't see any reason for her to change...unless you know something you're not telling me."

"We talked, Dad."

"About what?"

"Why don't you ask Ellie?"

Sam shook out his paper, but not like a man looking forward to the ease of the grave. Not at all like that. He gave it the vigorous, mad-as-hell shake of a man feeling his sap rise for the first time in years.

C.J. held her book in front of her face so he wouldn't see her trying not to laugh, so he wouldn't see the devilish delight she took in rattling the doors of his self-made prison.

She tried to get her mind back on lofty topics such as cows' udders and the number of gallons of milk they produced for the coffers of Mississippi's dairy farmers, but a few things got in the way, things such as remorse and a recently liberated libido.

"That Clint Garrett's a good writer," her daddy said, and she jumped as if he'd been reading her mind.

"What do you mean?"

"What do you mean, what do I mean? I mean the young man has a talent for writing. I wonder what he's doing with a small-town paper."

"I'm sure I don't know."

Sam pulled his glasses down and gave her this *look*. "Well, I didn't ask you. I just made a statement. What's bothering you?"

"Nothing."

He snapped the paper twice and glared at her. "All right then."

C.J. got up and went to the kitchen where she consoled herself with three crackers loaded with peanut butter.

What *was* Clint Garrett doing?

Wads of paper littered the floor around Clint's desk. He plucked another page off his printer, crumpled it up and lobbed it toward the wastebasket. It hit the rim, bounced off and landed on the floor amongst the rest of the rejected paper.

"Seven out of seven," he said. "Not bad."

"What's this?" Wayne pulled up a chair, then propped his feet on Clint's desk.

"Basketball practice."

Wayne surveyed the mess. "Tell me that's not the story I'm counting on running in tomorrow's paper."

"That's it."

"Why?"

"It's a piece of garbage."

Wayne leaned over and started picking it up and smoothing the pages flat. "I'll be the judge of that. What's eating you anyway?"

C. J. Maxey. ''Nothing.''

''It doesn't look like *nothing* to me. It looks like a plain old case of the blues.''

''Even scoundrels get the blues.''

The clock on his desk said half past nine, thirty minutes till doom. He kicked back, picked up his helmet and saluted his boss.

''You off to cover the dairy princess?''

That's all it took to send his flag waving at full mast, just the mention of that vixen in demure pink panties. He turned sideways so Wayne wouldn't notice.

''Yep, I'm off to *cover* the princess.''

Forget honor. Forget scruples. This time he would show no mercy.

He stomped out of the office and jumped on his Harley, prepared to head toward the fairgrounds where members of the 4-H Club would be showing their dairy cows and the farmers would be gathered for a lecture on the rising costs of milk production.

''Another fun-packed day in the life of an ace reporter.''

The old blue tick that sometimes rode shotgun in Wayne's pickup truck took one look at Clint, tucked his tail between his legs and slunk off.

''Even dogs can't stand me.''

Clint revved his engine and was roaring toward his destination when he changed his mind and headed toward a little yellow cottage on the outskirts of town. If he was going to be in the same place as the indomitable Miss Maxey, he might as well throw her off-balance before she did it to him first.

What would she be wearing today? Something provocative, no doubt, in spite of the fact that she'd be tromping around a dairy barn with its mine field of gifts from nervous cows.

He parked his bike, then marched up her front steps to the beat of invisible war drums and rang the doorbell. He pictured C.J. coming to the door in a little outfit no bigger than a handkerchief.

This time he'd show her what happened to a man provoked beyond his capacity to endure. He'd teach her that it was not nice to tempt a man to the breaking point, tease him to the brink of insanity and then accuse *him* of being a cad.

"Hello," she said. "What brings you here?" She wore faded jeans and a white T-shirt.

Her megawatt smile didn't fool him, not for one minute.

"I just dropped by for a conjugal visit. Do I need to take a number and wait?"

There's nothing like watching a feisty woman work up a head of steam. First her face turned pink, then her eyes got bright and next her body looked electrified. A storm was brewing, and it was all fixing to wash over him. Clint braced for the onslaught.

And then she smiled, turning the tables so quickly he was left with his jaw hanging down and another smart remark dying on his tongue. The battle was only minutes old and already he was battered and bloody.

"I guess I deserve that after the way I behaved the other night." She smiled again, pouring salt all over his open wounds. "Or should I say misbehaved?"

Where was her sharp tongue when he needed it?

Where was her come-and-get-me dress? Where was her flash, her fire?

Here he was standing on her porch disarmed, a man who made his living with words and who couldn't think of a single biting word to say. One phrase was all he needed, one brilliant witty bit of repartee that would turn the winds of victory back in his direction.

"I came to offer you a ride to the dairy expo, but I see you're not dressed yet."

He couldn't believe he'd said that. She had him so confused he was acting almost normal. If he didn't soon get out of town she'd have him hogtied in button-down shirts and ties that featured navy-blue stripes. She'd have him civilized, sanitized and mortgaged. She'd have him *reformed*.

Chapter Ten

Clint strolled off her porch and mounted his big Harley. C.J. didn't breathe till he'd roared down her driveway and was on the open road.

She was on such an adrenaline high she could barely stand still. Any other time she'd have raced across the yard and through the hedge to tell Sandi, but too much misunderstanding stood between them.

C.J. went back inside. Sam was stretched on the kitchen floor with his head under the sink.

"Dad? I'm ready to go to the Expo."

"Fine." He didn't even stick his head out.

"I thought you were going."

"I changed my mind."

Was this a good thing or a bad thing? Probably a little of both. Obviously he was avoiding Ellie, who would definitely be there, but also he was fixing a faucet that had leaked for three years. Showing a little interest in things around the house. Showing a little life, a little spunk.

"Okay," she said. "I'll see you later."

"Have fun."

"I will. I'll tell Ellie you said hello."

Sam came out from under the sink so fast he banged his head. "You'll do no such thing."

"Why?"

"If Ellie wanted to say hello, she'd have come here and said it in person."

"It works both ways, Dad."

He gave her another of his famous *looks,* then disappeared under the sink. "I'm busy here," he said.

"Okay, then. If you change your mind, come on down. We'll be at the Expo about two hours."

Blake Dix was his name. Clint had inquired. What was a man like that doing at the Expo anyway? You'd think a man who worked at a church would know better than to practically maul a woman in public.

To make matters worse, C.J. didn't seem to be minding all that much. She was sitting on a bale of hay soaking up every word that fell from Dix's lips.

"Where have you been all my life, C.J.?"

Dix's line was the oldest pickup in the world. Stale as last week's bread.

"Right under your nose," she said with a good deal of spunk and more than a little stinger.

Clint took heart from that, but not much. Especially since the Dix masher leaned over and twirled a wisp of her hair between his sleazy fingers and she seemed inclined to let him.

"Just think of all the time we wasted, C.J."

She slapped his hand out of her hair. "Go chase some *pretty* girls, Blake. I have more important things to do than canoodle with you."

"I'm dying here, C.J."

Clint almost felt sorry for the fool. Dix actually thought he could get past her lethal stinger. The consequences weren't long in coming.

"Go sing a dirge. Maybe that'll revive you."

C.J. launched herself off the hay and left Dix standing there wondering if his deodorant had failed him.

Clint wanted to give a rebel yell, but grabbed a handful of cotton candy cones instead.

"What are you doing here, as if it's not perfectly obvious?" C.J. stood like a female Patton, hands on her hips, a take-no-prisoners look in her eyes.

"Having a little snack."

"Five cones of cotton candy?"

"I like sugar." He stared deliberately at her berry-colored lips and watched the flush come into her cheeks. He was beginning to feel more like himself. Heck, he was beginning to have fun again.

"Want some?" he said, making it perfectly clear he wasn't talking about cotton candy.

"Why don't you ask a more appreciative audience? I see her coming right now."

"What in the hell do you mean by that?" he yelled, but the devilish Crystal Jean Maxey had already sashayed away toward the dairy barn.

"What's going on?"

He wheeled around to see Sandi Wentworth standing at his elbow. Any man in his right mind would have been thrilled by this turn of events. Exit a heart-less woman, enter a woman who was all heart.

It said more than he cared to know about his state of mind that he pined for vinegar when he could have sugar.

"I don't know," he said. "You tell me."

C.J. told herself if she looked back she'd turn to a pillar of salt. Like Lot's wife. Like every other woman who didn't heed all the warning signs.

She hastened into the dairy barn and searched the crowd for Ellie. Where was she? The program would be starting in fifteen minutes. It wasn't like her to be late. Maybe she was sick. But wouldn't she have called?

C.J. reached into her shoulder bag and pulled out her cell phone.

"Ellie? You sound terrible. Are you sick?"

"Allergies."

Ellie'd never had allergies that C.J. knew of, but she didn't contradict her. "The show's about to start. I thought you were coming."

"I have lots of catching up to do at work. Is Sam with you?"

"No."

"Give me twenty minutes. I'll be there."

"Ellie…"

"What?"

"It's working."

"What's working?"

"Absence is making the heart grow fonder. Dad's been a bear."

Ellie snorted. "It's not his heart. It's indigestion."

"We'll see." Out of the corner of her eye C.J. saw Sandi coming. "I have to go, Ellie."

She ducked across two rows of chairs that had been set up for today's events. If she could just make it around the corner of the makeshift stage she'd be all right: she'd be out of sight.

"C.J., wait."

Caught. Sandi looked flushed and out of breath, and C.J. wondered how much of it was from the exertion of trying to catch her and how much was due to the attentions of a certain sexy reporter. She couldn't say his name to herself, couldn't even *think* it without getting weak in the knees.

"I've been trying to reach you." C.J. didn't say anything. What was there to say? "I knew I'd find you here. We need to talk."

"About what?"

"Oh, C.J. Don't. We have nothing to fight about."

"You're right. We certainly don't."

The county's biggest dairy farmer, Walter Crumpett, walked onstage and began to fiddle with the microphone. High-pitched squealing noises filled the barn and a couple of cows started mooing.

Reprieved. "I have to go." C.J. started around to the back of the stage but Sandi caught her arm.

"Nothing happened between us," Sandi said. "All Clint did was ask questions about *you.*"

Sandi had never lied to her. C.J. wanted to believe, but still...

"Don't you see, C.J.? It's *you* he wants, not me."

"I have to go."

"C.J...."

Years of friendship loomed large and suddenly C.J.

wondered how she'd ever been foolish enough to let one little misunderstanding come between them.

"I believe you, Sandi. Come over tonight and we'll eat popcorn and watch Clark Gable."

C.J. hugged her oldest and best friend in the whole world. "I'm sorry, Sandi."

"Hush, hush. You're making me cry." Onstage Walter Crumpett paged C.J. over the ornery microphone. "Knock 'em dead, C.J."

"I'll be satisfied if I can keep them awake."

Waiting backstage to be announced, C.J. knew she should be thinking about the speech she was about to deliver. Instead she thought about Clint Garrett cozied up in the bar plying her best friend with questions. It would have been a very hopeful sign if C.J. didn't know that the woman Clint had inquired about was not she but a make-believe woman, a trumped-up glamour queen who didn't even exist.

Maybe he was interested in that woman, interested enough to steal a few kisses in the meadow and take her home for a brief fling.

They say be careful what you wish for because you just might get it. It looked as if C.J. had received what she wished for—excess.

Sure, it was fun and exciting, heady stuff for a plain country girl who had no *wild* days of youth to recall and whose social whirl consisted of having five dollars bid on her fried chicken at the church's box supper.

All of a sudden she realized she wanted more, she wanted *real* love, the kind where a man loved you exactly as you were and loved you completely. The kind where a man kissed the back of your neck in the evening and said, "Let me give you a massage, darling." The kind where a man cherished everything about you.

The kind where you loved him right back in exactly the same totally accepting, all-encompassing way.

An announcement filtered through her preoccupation. "And now here she is...Lee County's Dairy Princess...Crystal Jean Maxey!"

C.J. smoothed her jeans, made sure her T-shirt was tucked in, then climbed the rickety steps of the makeshift stage. The audience was sparse, a few dairy farmers, some she knew, some she didn't, along with a handful of wives who had come along because any outing, even one to a smelly old dairy barn, was better than none.

Ellie was in the audience giving her a thumbs-up smile, but Sam wasn't there. C.J. had half expected him to change his mind and come. Except for the few times he'd had an emergency in the clinic, he'd never failed to show support for his daughter.

Not that she was upset, not by a long shot. In fact, she took his absence as a good omen, a sign that at last Sam was becoming whole again.

Sitting beside Ellie was Sandi, and lounging in the back was Clint, camera slung on his hip and a sardonic grin on his face.

"Ladies and gentlemen," she said. "I feel like Eve without her fig leaf. Cast into a situation I'm totally unfamiliar with, being a princess."

Winning her audience with laughter was heady. It gave C.J. the courage she needed to launch into the heart of her speech—promoting the dairy industry.

Chapter Eleven

Clint didn't know who that was on the stage, but it certainly wasn't C. J. Maxey, at least not the one he knew. The smart, articulate, unadorned woman onstage was not somebody he would *ever* offer a *conjugal visit*. The woman onstage was the kind you carried hothouse roses to, the kind you didn't mess around with usually, because they were way out of your league. Shoot, she was the kind of woman you'd take fishing…if you got really serious.

The thing was, he *wanted* to buy roses for this woman. He wanted to grow two sizes taller so he'd be worthy of being seen with her on his arm. Hell, he was about a hair's breadth from inviting her to go fishing.

He should leave. Right this minute.

But that would be a cowardly act, and anyhow he

was only going to be in town a few weeks longer, just long enough to cover the princess all the way to the state pageant. He could certainly hold out against this interesting, intelligent, straightforward woman that long.

Look on the bright side, the way she changed chameleon-like from day to day, she'd probably metamorphose into somebody else tomorrow, maybe even somebody down on his level.

The audience gave her a standing ovation. Clint felt as if he'd personally wooed and won the crowd. When she smiled and waved, he thought she was looking directly at him.

Walter Crumpett pranced back onstage and brayed into the microphone, "Let's give her another round of applause, folks…our own dairy princess. Wasn't she wonderful?"

The audience showed their agreement by stomping and clapping. That Dix character who was still hanging around made a complete jackass of himself.

"And now, folks," Crumpett said, "we come to that part of the show where you can win a chance to have your picture taken with the princess. Bring 'em on, Jack."

Two black-and-white Holstein cows topped the ramp and clomped onstage switching their tails and chewing their cuds. "There they are, folks," Crumpett yelled, "Bossy and Jane, two fresh milk cows. Now who wants to try their hand at milking? Come on, boys, don't be shy."

Dix was the first one onstage. He was the most determined fellow Clint had ever seen, and it didn't surprise him one bit when Dix won the milking contest.

Clint moved to the stage to get a shot of the winner, and what happened next couldn't have been better if he'd scripted it himself.

The princess took her place beside Dix who behaved himself long enough for the cameras to click off several shots. Then temptation overcame him. He eased an arm behind C.J. and grabbed a handful of her cute little bottom. Still smiling for the camera, C.J. reached back, grabbed his wrist and twisted.

Dix yowled and Bossy, who was right behind them, relieved herself in fright. C.J. twisted again and when Dix stepped backward, his fancy boots lost purchase and he went down with a thud.

"I guess you really fell for the princess," Crumpett yelled, and Dix said a word you couldn't print in a small-town family newspaper.

C.J. extended her hand to help him up, but Dix declined.

"Congratulations, Blake," she said. "You won."

Clint was going to send that woman roses.

"That was the funniest thing I've ever seen," Sandi said.

She and C.J. were sitting on the swing on C.J.'s front porch with a moon as big as Texas shining through the trees and music drifting through the open screen door.

"Served him right."

"It was the best comeuppance I've ever seen. He'll probably never get the smell out of his boots."

Their laughter lifted on the hot summer air and C.J. felt cleansed.

This is the way it should be, she thought. Good friends, always there, loving and supporting, understanding and forgiving.

"That music's too good to sit still," C.J. said, and she and Sandi jumped up and began to jitterbug.

Sam came smiling to the door. "Looks like you two are having fun," he said.

"We are. Come out and join us, Dad."

"No, I thought I'd take a little ride."

"Where're you going?"

"Over to Ellie's. Don't wait up for me."

They watched until he got into his pickup truck.

"He looked ten years younger," Sandi said. "What do you think's going on?"

"I think he's going courting."

"Good. Turn up the music."

C.J. turned it to ear-splitting volume and they began to boogie once more.

"May I have this dance?" Clint Garrett was standing on the front porch steps with the moonlight in his impossibly black hair and a dozen long-stemmed pink roses in his hand.

"How did you do that?" C.J. asked. "I didn't even hear your motorcycle."

"I have my Corvette."

Sure enough, a sleek black Corvette convertible of ancient vintage was parked underneath the magnolia tree. C.J. turned to ask Sandi if she'd heard him drive up, but her friend had vanished through the hedge that separated their houses.

Clint held out the roses.

"For me?"

"Yes. The color reminded me of your cheeks."

It was the most romantic thing any man had ever said to her. C.J. felt like lolling back on the swing in a full-blown swoon.

"Thank you." She buried her face in the fragrant blossoms and bit her tongue to keep from asking *why*. Tonight was not the time for a sharp tongue and a stinging wit. Tonight was the time for moonlight and magic.

"They're my way of saying *I'm sorry*," he said.

"So am I. For...everything."

They looked at each other as if they'd never met, strangers vividly aware of each other. The boogie gave way to a romantic ballad.

Clint held out his arms and C.J. laid her roses in the swing then moved into them as naturally as if that's where she'd always belonged. Her head fit exactly right against his shoulder, his arms fit perfectly around her waist, her hips matched his hips as if they'd been designed to meld together in a romantic dance in the moonlight on a soft summer night.

"We fit," he said, echoing exactly what she was thinking.

"Yes."

He moved a fraction closer and C.J. saw how it would be possible to fall in love in an instant without even trying. She saw how it was possible to forget reason and listen entirely to the heart.

She closed her eyes and rested her head on a shoulder so broad and strong it could keep a woman safe no matter what. He smelled faintly of soap, and of soft summer wind. She could die of happiness right now.

"We dance well together," he said, as if he were surprised.

She wasn't. She guessed she'd known all along that whatever she and Clint Garrett did together, they'd do it with a compatibility that was surely shaped by fate.

"I've never danced with a man," she said. In high school she was always the wallflower, the one left to pour the punch while other girls whirled around the dance floor.

"Never?"

"I guess I was waiting for you."

He tangled his hands in her hair and tilted her head so he could gaze into her eyes. "And I guess I was waiting for you."

She'd never seen anything as beautiful as his eyes, never felt anything as wonderful as his lips, never known anything as magical as the kiss that transformed her from ordinary to special. Of all the women in the universe, she was most blessed.

Chapter Twelve

The woman in his arms was soft and sweet, yet another facet of the ever-changing, endlessly fascinating C. J. Maxey. Clint had thought he'd kiss her lightly in a casual sort of way, a let's-make-up-and-be-friends sort of way. But the way it all ended up surprised him out of his socks. Even a man as jaded and devil-may-care as he knew when a kiss was special. This one topped the scale. It sent him over the moon, and that's where he stayed.

There was no way he could let go of her, no way he could stop kissing her. He pulled her closer, molding their bodies together in a fit as perfect as any he'd ever known.

He wanted her as he'd wanted no other woman. The porch swing beckoned, and he eased her back onto the cushions.

She was in shorts. Her legs were bare. Her T-shirt was a small barrier, easily dispensed.

With the small wanting sounds of a woman on the edge, she wrapped arms and legs around him, urging him closer. It would be so easy to take what he wanted.

No, more than wanted. He needed C. J. Maxey and that scared him.

In addition, a latent honor reared its aggravating head, and he knew he could never take this woman casually. He could never take his pleasure then simply walk away.

Why hadn't he sent the roses instead of bringing them in person?

He broke contact and eased back a fraction so he could see her face. Mistake. Softened by moonlight and kisses, she was the most appealing woman he'd ever seen.

It took Herculean effort to stop.

"C.J.….."

"Hmm?"

Why did her eyes have to be so bright? Her smile so tender?

"Is your dad here?"

"No. He won't be back till late. Maybe not at all."

Clearly, it was an invitation. One he was a fool to ignore and a bigger fool to accept. He was treading on thin ice here, in great danger of falling through.

"There's something I have to ask you," he said.

There were lots of things he needed to know about her. For instance, what did she do for fun? Sit inside and kill her brain cells with TV? Mince around a shopping mall looking for bargains? Eat food with unpronounceable names at expensive restaurants when there was a good mom-and-pop establishment just down the road that served peas and cornbread?

"Yes?" she said, "What did you want to ask me?"

"Will you go fishing with me?"

C.J. didn't hear Sam when she got up the next morning, so she went outside looking for him. He was on the back porch with his bare feet up on the rail, drinking coffee and reading the newspaper.

"What time did you get in last night?" she asked.

"What kind of question is that to ask your father?"

"You didn't answer."

"None of your business."

"That's your answer?"

"Yep." He went back to his paper, grinning.

"It looks like you had fun."

"Yep."

"What's with this *yep*. You sound like some TV character from Podunk, USA."

"Can't a man be in a good mood without facing an inquisition from a nosy daughter?"

"Nosy? You're calling me nosy? And don't you dare say *yep*."

"If the shoe fits…"

"I guess I'll have to ask Ellie."

"You do that."

He grinned some more, then whistled an old tune. He already had his head buried in the paper before C.J. recognized it. Her insouciant dad was whistling "Making Whoopee."

C.J. was so tickled she was bouncing on the balls

of her feet the way she'd done when she was a little girl and excitement got the best of her.

Sam studied her over the tops of his glasses. "What are you doing dressed like that?"

"I'm going fishing after a while."

"Dressed like that?"

Maybe she'd gone overboard. The shorts were fine, maybe a little on the skimpy side, but still she *did* have nice legs, so what did it hurt to show them off to the right man? And Clint Garrett was exactly the right man. After last night's kiss on the front porch, she was absolutely certain of that.

"What do you mean, dressed like that?"

"What's that little thing around your—" he indicated his chest "—you call that a blouse?"

"No, it's a tube top."

"Mosquitoes will eat you up."

She was hoping to be nibbled by a more exciting predator.

"I'm taking repellant."

He eyed her top once more. "I don't think they make repellant for that. Better put on a shirt, C.J."

Suddenly she saw herself through her dad's eyes, a young woman showing every inch of skin she could without parading around stark naked. A young woman obviously on the make.

C.J. sighed. You'd think she'd have learned her lesson by now. All that posturing around in falsies and provocative clothing had sent out the wrong signals.

If she wanted a repeat of exactly what had already happened with Clint, all she had to do was show up at the front door dressed fit to seduce. She'd get exactly what she deserved: a man who used her and went his merry way.

In the last few weeks she'd experienced both excess and romance, and she'd stand up in a court of law and testify that she'd take romance every time.

What she really wanted was to be *loved*, not for who somebody thought she was but for who she *really* was.

"You're right, Dad. I'd better put on a shirt."

She started into the house and her dad called after her.

"C.J.?" When she turned around he had the sweetest look on his face, like a man who'd awakened from a long nightmare to discover life was wonderful after all.

"You really like Ellie, don't you?"

"Yes, Dad. I *love* Ellie."

He smiled. "I thought so." He started to immerse himself in the paper once more, then added, "Who're you going fishing with?"

"Clint Garrett."

"Oh? Okay, have a good time."

"Thanks, Dad. I plan to."

And she did. Oh, she did.

When Clint saw C.J. he knew he was in trouble. Here was a woman who took her fishing seriously. Jeans for sitting on the creek bank, long-sleeved shirt so her arms wouldn't blister, sturdy shoes just right for wading muddy fishing holes, baseball cap angled low to protect her eyes.

"I see you've fished before."

"Dad and I used to go all the time."

"Used to?"

She hesitated before she answered as if she were weighing her words. When she finally spoke he saw the naked truth in her eyes.

"Yes. Before the accident. Mom was an invalid for three years before she died. I was driving."

"I'm sorry. That had to be hard. You weren't much more than a kid."

"How did you know?"

"Sandi."

"Oh."

"I hope you don't mind."

"No. No, I don't mind. In fact, it feels good to talk to you about it."

"Talk about it all you want. I'll listen."

"Okay, I just might."

She smiled that open, trusting smile that made him feel like he ought to be clanking around in a suit of armor and rescuing damsels in distress. He took the picnic basket and then escorted her to the Corvette.

"I'm glad you left the top down." She climbed in and flashed her wonderful smile again. "I've never ridden in one of these before."

"Corvette or convertible?"

"Neither."

"It looks like you're having all your firsts with me."

He spoke in a casual manner, but it didn't feel casual at all, this heady knowledge that he was giving C.J. new experiences, all of them romantic. He walked to the driver's side feeling ten feet tall. How many more firsts could he give C. J. Maxey?

* * *

On any given summer's day you could see fishermen on the Tennessee/Tombigbee Waterway, lined up along grassy sloping banks, casting from the small boats that drifted in the eddies, standing on the sides of the bridges watching corks bobbing in the water.

Clint chose a less populated fishing spot, a little creek really, one so small it didn't even have a name that C.J. knew of, and she knew just about every creek in Lee County, for fishing had once been her dad's favorite pastime.

"This looks like a good spot." Clint parked the car underneath a giant hickory tree. Shells from last fall's crop of nuts still littered the ground and they made nice crunching sounds when she walked on them.

He'd brought all the fishing supplies, and it was an impressive array.

"I brought some live bait," he said. "I'll help you bait your hook."

"Are you kidding?"

"You bait your own?"

"Yes. Dad didn't teach me to be a spectator. He taught me to *fish*."

Clint laughed. "Sounds like a challenge to me. What do you want to bet I catch the most fish?"

"I'll wager the wishbone."

"You fried a chicken? The old-fashioned way?"

"Yes. I'll have you know this is a country girl you're talking to, mister."

"You're on."

They left for the creek bank laughing. Clint didn't bother to raise the top or lock the car. There was no one around for miles.

C.J. loved walking in the woods. She loved the cool

green silence, the surprise of woodland flowers, the occasional flash of wings as cardinals and bluejays and mockingbirds dived toward unsuspecting bugs. Such beauty called for reverence, and she walked without shattering the cathedral-like hush with chatter.

She liked to fish the same way, with a minimum of talk and a maximum of effort. By the time they stopped for lunch she had six fish on her stringer, Clint had four.

"You won," he said.

He seemed pleased about her victory, even jovial.

"I like you this way," she told him.

"What way?"

"Honest."

"I like you this way, too."

"How?"

"Honest." He smiled, then handed her the piece of chicken called the wishbone. "Looks good."

"Eat it, then."

"No, you won. Fair's fair."

"You have the meat, I get the wish."

"A man could get addicted to fishing like this."

"So could a girl."

Their eyes got tangled up, and C.J. wondered if he would kiss her. She wanted him to. Wanted it with a heart-thumping, breath-stopping urgency that was almost palpable.

Instead he took a bite of fried chicken then closed his eyes and moaned. It sounded sexual to C.J., but then around Clint the least little thing became sexual.

"Make a wish," he said, finally, handing her the wishbone.

Closing her eyes, she wrapped her little finger around one end of the bone and he caught the other. The bone snapped.

"What did you wish?" he asked.

"It won't come true if you tell."

"That's an old wives' tale."

"Really?"

"Yes. How can it come true if you *don't* tell, especially if you don't tell the dreammaker."

Oh, she loved it, this playful mood of his, this teasing, flirtatious, generous-hearted mood that made her believe she was somebody special.

"Promise you won't laugh," she said.

"I solemnly swear. Scout's honor."

"You were a boy scout?"

"No, but I always wanted to be."

"Okay, that's good enough for me."

"Is it?"

Something about his voice caught her high under her breastbone and wouldn't let go. Tender feelings flowed through her like a river, and she reached out and caught his hand.

"Yes," she whispered. "It's *perfect* for me."

There now. She hoped she'd made up in some small way for the way she'd turned on him the night he rescued her, the night of the green monkeys.

"Tell me your wish, C.J." The tenderness in his tone wrapped around her like a warm hug.

"I always wondered what it would be like to go skinny-dipping." The ghost of a smile played around his lips. "You said you wouldn't laugh."

"I'm not. I'm thinking that a woman who caught

six fish ought to be granted that one simple wish."
He smiled at her. "Today, as a matter of fact."

She glanced at the quiet green water. A canopy of
trees shaded their fishing spot, and farther down-
stream a still section reflected the sun-drenched sky.
She imagined how the water would feel closing over
her naked skin. Wet and warm and silky. Sensual.
Like being flooded with love.

"If only I could," she said.

"You not only can, you *will*."

Clint stowed the dishes in the picnic basket, then
hung the quilt on the branches of the hickory tree.

"What are you doing?"

"Making you a cabana." He smiled at her. "For
privacy."

A few days ago he'd have seized the opportunity
for sport. He'd have stripped off his clothes and
waded in, calling for her to join him, promising to
close his eyes then going back on his promise.

"What about you?" she asked.

"I sometimes enjoy a nap after lunch…in the car."

"Oh."

Disappointment battled pleasure, with pleasure finally winning. Men like Clint didn't do heroic things
like this every day. Instinctively she knew that. The
gift was rare indeed.

"You can give a yell if you need me."

"Thank you, Clint." She stood on tiptoes and
kissed him softly on the mouth. "I think you're my
hero."

Chapter Thirteen

Clint stretched in the back seat of the car with his arms folded under his head and his ear tuned to the distant sounds from the creek.

He pictured C.J. romping in the water, hair slicked back, moisture beaded on her skin, nipples puckered by the slight chill of the spring-fed creek. Sitting there in the car missing all the fun he had to be the world's biggest fool. Or hero.

That's what she'd called him. Her hero. A warm glow settled somewhere in the region of his heart and wouldn't let go no matter how hard he tried.

A man could get used to being a hero. A man could grow accustomed to being held in high regard by a lovely, intelligent woman. A man could even make a few changes for a woman like that.

If he wanted to.

"I'm out of the water," C.J. called.

"Are you decent?" he called back, knowing full well she was.

The C.J. he'd brought to the creek bank today was the kind of girl his mother would have picked for him. She was the kind of girl his mother would have taken to her Saturday Sewing Circle and introduced proudly to all her friends. She was the kind of girl his mother would have bragged about to the postman, the grocer and anybody else who would listen.

"Mostly," she yelled back. "Except for a few wet patches here and there."

His mouth went dry thinking of those wet spots. "I'll be right there."

C.J. was standing beside the stream with her hair plastered to her head and her shirt clinging to dampened skin that still glowed from the cool water. She'd taken the patchwork quilt off the tree, and it dangled from her hand.

"Thank you for that lovely swim."

"You're more than welcome."

They faced each other with perfect stillness. Afterward he would never remember who made the first move, but suddenly they were in each other's arms.

The touch of her lips seared his soul. That was the only way he could describe what was happening. He'd never felt anything like this.

If he'd tried to explain it, he would have failed. All he knew was that he was completely lost. There was no more Clint Garrett, a man alone viewing the world through jaded eyes. There was simply an ego that disappeared and left in its place a beating heart.

His blood sang with awareness, his body clamored for release.

With sexy little murmurings, C.J. indicated she felt the same way. It would be so easy to lower her to the quilt and find release in her sweet supple body on a hot summer's day.

But he wanted more. He wanted to keep this special something that sizzled between them. He wanted to feed the fire slowly, to coax the flame gradually until it burned so hot the embers would never die.

"Clint, please…" C.J. wove her hands into the front of his shirt and tangled her fingers in his chest hair. "I want…I need…"

"So do I, sweetheart. So do I. But I want it to be just right."

He wanted to remain her hero. He didn't want her to ever wake up in the morning and say, my goodness, what have I done? He didn't want her to call Sandi and say, that scoundrel took me on the creekbank like an alley cat.

Why he wanted more, he couldn't say. Maybe it had to do with finally living up to his mother's expectations. Maybe it had to do with C.J. herself, the one woman who bested and intrigued him at every turn. And so he gentled her with tender kisses and soft caresses until she lay against his chest, sighing.

"We'd better be getting back," he said.

"I suppose so."

Her reluctance thrilled him. He wanted C.J. to want him more than she'd ever wanted anything in her life.

Tomorrow maybe he'd change his mind. Maybe he'd get on his Harley and leave Hot Coffee and never look back. But today he wanted this: her sweet lips and her tender regard.

She stood on tiptoe and kissed him on the mouth, softly. "Thank you for a beautiful day."

It was enough. For now, it was enough.

C.J. was in such an overwrought state of jangled nerves and raging libido that she slipped in the back door so she wouldn't have to say anything to Sam. She eased her bedroom door shut, then lay on the bed with her body tingling and her heart on fire.

She could hear Sam in the kitchen whistling.

At least somebody's satisfied. Not that she was envious. She was happy for her father. She really was.

Right now what she needed was her mother, somebody she could go to and say, tell me what to do when you think you're falling in love and you're not sure the man feels the same way. Do you act pushy and try to get what you want? Do you wait and hope he catches on? Do you retreat? Advance? Play hard to get? Don't play games at all but be brutally honest even if it means you make a fool of yourself? Even if it drives him away?

C.J. couldn't bear the thought of driving Clint away, especially now, especially since she'd caught a glimpse of the real man.

Sam knocked on her door. "C.J., I thought I heard a car. Are you in there?"

"Yes."

"Want some iced tea?"

"No thanks, Dad."

"What about supper? I'm making tuna salad."

''Maybe I'll get a sandwich when I come back. I thought I'd go over to Ellie's.''

There was a long silence, then Sam said, ''She's busy tonight.''

''How do you know?''

''I'm taking her to the movies.'' You could drive a Mack truck through the long pause. ''Uh, C.J....don't wait up for me.''

''Dad, I'm not going to be checking the clock. Okay?''

''Right.''

He walked back down the hall like Fred Astaire tap dancing.

C.J. must have dozed, because it was dark outside and she was still lying on top of her bed with her wrinkled fishing clothes on. She listened to the no one's-home silence. Sam had already gone.

She shucked her clothes, put on fresh shorts and a T-shirt and went outside. Crickets and cicadas joined in an evening symphony typical of Mississippi on a humid summer night. She lingered a while on the front porch listening, then went to the hedge that separated her house from Sandi's.

She had to talk to somebody.

A thorny wild rose growing in the hedge caught the edge of her shorts and she had to stop to untangle herself. Still held captive by briars she heard the unmistakable roar of a Harley.

Clint. Her heart beat double time and she held her breath as the beam of light moved closer.

He was coming to see her. She tried to hurry the process of freeing herself and only succeeded in getting further trapped.

Oh, lord, would he think she wasn't home and leave? Would he knock on her door, see the light she'd left on in her bedroom and think she didn't want to come to the door?

She grabbed the prickly branch and scratched her hand and arm.

"Drat!"

A bright light illuminated the hedge, and C.J. felt like a rabbit caught in a trap. She was getting all set to wave and yell when the Harley turned into Sandi's driveway.

Knives sliced C.J.'s heart. A giant hand squeezed all the breath out of her chest. The Tombigbee River flooded her throat and choked her.

Clint was now halfway up Sandi's driveway. C.J. felt betrayed...and pitiful. Lord, she must *look* pitiful. What if he saw her like that?

Worse, what if he saw her at all and thought she was spying? C.J. hunkered down, trying to hide behind the sparse section of hedge and a spindly wild rose. Thorns raked across her cheek and she bit her lip to keep from crying out.

Clint left his bike underneath a magnolia tree and rang the doorbell. Sandi came to the door all smiles, then reached out and pulled Clint inside and the door closed behind them.

C.J. jerked free of the brambles and left a long scratch along her thigh. All in all, the only positive thing she could say about the evening was that Clint hadn't been carrying flowers.

"Thank you for seeing me on such short notice," Clint told Sandi.

"I'm not sure it's such a good idea. I'm still not convinced I shouldn't have told her."

"I want it to be a surprise."

"Surprises sometimes have a way of backfiring."

"I'll take my chances."

A good hunk of cheese and a box of crackers sat on the low table in front of the sofa along with two bottles of chilled beer.

"I never did learn the art of fine entertaining," she said.

"This is just right."

It was amazing how excitement made a man hungry. He savored a big hunk of cheese before turning to Sandi.

"Now," he said, "here's what I want from you."

Chapter Fourteen

"Good lord, what happened to you?"

Blake Dix posed in the doorway of the church's office as if he'd never taken a public dive into cow manure.

"Had a fight with a wild rose. I lost."

"Yeah. You look like you could use a little tender loving care." He smiled. "I'm good at that."

"I'm sure you are, Blake...with the right woman."

"If you're saying you're not the right woman, I wish you'd give me a chance to change your mind."

"Thanks, but no."

"Look, C.J., about the other day. I know I acted like a fool. I'm not usually like that. I want to apologize."

"Apology accepted. And, Blake, you just went up three notches in my estimation."

"I'll see what I can do to gain a few more." He laid a stack of papers on her desk. "I won't need these till the day after tomorrow. No sense making you stay late just because I'm too lazy to get it to you." He waggled his eyebrows. "How'd I do that time?"

Making an upward motion with her thumbs she said, "Another notch."

They were laughing when a young man from Pete's Gifts and Florals knocked on the door frame.

"Are you Miss Crystal Jean Maxey?"

"I am."

"Sign here, please," he said, then stepped into the hall and came back with an enormous heart-shaped candy box plus a three-foot cardboard valentine with "Be Mine!" embossed in gold letters.

"Wow!" Blake hefted the candy box. "How much chocolate do you suppose is in there?"

"Ten pounds," the delivery boy said. "Biggest one we've got." He tipped his hat. "Have a nice day, ma'am."

"Who's sending you Valentine's gifts in June?"

C.J. wasn't certain, but she could dream, couldn't she? Blake walked around the cardboard valentine, viewing it from all sides.

"'Your Secret Admirer'" he read. "Clever. Wish I'd thought of it."

"Do you mind? This is private."

C.J. stowed the huge valentine on her side of the desk, right beside her chair so she could see it every time she glanced that way.

"Aren't you going to share that candy? I have a

sweet tooth, you know. It's the curse of choir direc-
tors.''

"Sure." C.J. examined the box on all sides before
she opened it, hoping she'd find a card taped somewhere. But there was nothing. All she had to go by
was the signature on the valentine. It had to be Clint,
didn't it?

"Dig in," she said. "I'll just put the box over here
on the credenza and you can help yourself any time."

"You know you're going to be the most popular
person on the staff."

"Well, hey, you know me. I'll do anything for
fame."

"Right on, dairy princess."

Blake grabbed another handful of chocolate on the
way out the door, and C.J. picked up the sheaf of
papers he'd left with the full intention of applying
herself to her work. No sense going off into a fantasy
because she'd received chocolates.

She typed only one paragraph before the valentine
demanded her attention. There it was, all three feet of
it, the only valentine she'd ever received from an admirer, secret or otherwise.

Another first.

That's when she knew the identity of the sender—
Clint Garrett, who wanted to give her *firsts*.

C.J. picked up the phone and dialed.

"Sandi? I'd give you three guesses about what the
delivery boy brought, but I bet you already know."

"How do you know?"

"I saw Clint at your house last night."

"Shoot. I was afraid of that. Look, C.J., it was all
perfectly innocent...."

C.J. laughed. "I've learned my lesson. You don't have a betraying bone in your body."

"He only wanted to know some things about you, what you like, what you might have missed."

"You didn't tell him *everything,* I hope."

"Of course not, silly. A woman needs to preserve a certain air of mystery. A man likes to discover these things for himself."

"Is that what I've been preserving? My mystery?" C.J. sighed. "Sandi, what if it turns out he just wants to go exploring and I want more?"

"You're asking the woman who has had more failed trips to the altar than the law allows?"

"Well, yeah…"

"I don't know. Just follow your heart, I guess."

"You think so?"

"I read this great romance novel and that's what it said." Sandi sighed. "Phoebe always knew what to do. I sure miss her, don't you?"

A sweet nostalgia for the woman who had been both her mother and her friend washed over C.J.…and with it the guilt.

"Every day of my life."

"Maybe you could talk to Ellie."

"Maybe. Hey, Sandi, do you think Clint's going to call?"

"I'd bet money on it."

He didn't call. He was waiting on her doorstep when she got home. Her dad's truck was gone, and Clint sat on the front porch swing playing a harmonica.

"What happened?" He leaped up and cupped her face. "Are you all right?"

"I'm fine, but you ought to see that tiger I whipped." His hands felt so good on her face, so very good that she didn't want to move for the next hundred years. "I didn't know you played the blues harp. I *love* that music."

"It's just a little something I do to pass the time."

His hands were still on her face, thumbs making lazy circles around her mouth. She was in great danger of melting.

"Thank for the valentine and the candy."

"You knew?"

"Yes. Immediately."

Was he going to kiss her? It was right there in his eyes—desire, need.

The evening shadows fell across the porch in a patchwork of deep blue. Honeysuckle perfumed the air and cicadas sang of soft summer nights and sweet summer kisses.

Clint stepped back and C.J. pretended it didn't matter.

"I stopped by to invite you to the prom."

C.J. had to sit down. She was on the porch swing with Clint kneeling at her feet. She kept telling herself that, kept trying to hold on to that fact, but in her mind she was careening across Highway 78 with her mother crumpled in the passenger seat and a blood-soaked prom gown beside her.

"I've never been to a prom," she whispered.

"I know." His hands were warm on hers, but she still felt like ice. Any minute she was going to shatter.

"Sandi told me. She said the accident wasn't your fault, C.J."

"It felt like my fault. It still does."

"Maybe the prom wasn't a good idea. I won't mention it again."

"No, I want to go. I *need* to go."

"Good. Friday night then."

He was off the front porch and roaring away on his Harley before C.J. thought to invite him in. Why hadn't she invited him inside? They could have made sandwiches together then carried them out to the back deck and watched the moon rising over the lake.

He might have held her hand again. He might have cupped her face. He might have kissed her.

She would have kissed him right back. Then… Oh, and then, paradise.

Any fool with half sense and one eye could do what he was doing. That's what Clint decided as he sat in his office at eleven o'clock in the morning with his work already finished and time on his hands.

That's why he was spending so much time playing *hero* for C. J. Maxey. Too much idle time. As long as he kept the facts straight, everything would be all right. As long as he didn't start believing his own fiction, he could come out of this assignment none the worse for wear.

As long as C.J. was his assignment, he might as well have fun. Right? As long as she thought he was a hero, he might as well have a few laughs and act the part. Right?

"That's exactly why you should be someplace besides here." Wayne nodded toward the paperwork, then pulled up a chair and plopped an extra cup of coffee on Clint's desk. "You don't have enough to do at this paper. Never have, never will."

"I like it here."

"Is that why you're leaving? You like it so much?"

Clint hadn't thought about leaving for a few days. Actually he hadn't thought about it since he'd taken C.J. fishing. All of a sudden, his departure loomed large and he felt a huge emptiness in the pit of his stomach.

"You're always saying I should leave."

"Yeah, but I didn't mean Reform, Alabama."

"I don't know if I'll go there."

"Where're you going?"

"I haven't decided."

Wayne sipped his coffee for a while, then propped his feet on Clint's desk.

"Sounds like woman trouble to me."

"Bull."

Wayne laughed. "Wrong gender. Try *dairy princess.*"

"You're full of it, did you know that, Wayne?" Clint kicked back from his desk and picked up his helmet.

"Where're you going?"

"Thought I might scare up a story, being a crackerjack, top-notch, ace reporter."

With the wind at his back and seven hundred pounds of pure devil between his legs, Clint got his gumption back. Almost.

He still had to get through the prom.
And the state's dairy princess pageant.
Then he was leaving.
Maybe.

Chapter Fifteen

Clint and C.J. were the only ones at the prom. He'd transformed the ballroom at the Marriott in Shady Grove to an almost-perfect replica of a high school prom complete with a cut-glass punch bowl and streamers on the ceiling. Then he'd called some old college buddies with a band to come over and play while they danced.

Wearing the pink rose wrist corsage he'd given her and the blue prom dress she'd splurged on, C.J. felt sixteen again except it was better this time around. Much better. For one thing, the accident was no longer a gaping wound that bled on everything she did, but a fading scar. For another she had a date.

"You're the prettiest girl here," Clint told her and she laughed.

"I could say you're the handsomest man…except for the drummer."

"Rick may be cute but he can't dance." Clint executed some fancy footwork, then dipped her perilously low. "On the other hand, I make Fred Astaire look like a klutz."

"Since I'm keeping up with you, that must make me Ginger Rogers."

"My favorite dancing partner."

"You're full of flattery tonight."

Laughing, he spun her around till she was dizzy and had to sit down.

"I'll get you something to drink."

While she was sitting at the table it occurred to C.J. that he'd never responded to her remark about flattery. He might have said, It's the truth, which would have led naturally to a sweet kiss on the dance floor which might have led to something more.

But facts were facts, and C.J. had never been one to overlook the obvious. Clint was still who he was— an experienced, worldy wise man—and she was still who she was—a homely, plainspoken country girl.

"And never the twain shall meet," she whispered.

In spite of what Sandi had told her about being in love and following her heart, C.J. had no intention of taking that advice. After all, what did Sandi know? Look how many times she'd followed her heart, and she'd had it broken every time. Or at the very least, cracked a little bit.

C.J. didn't want her heart broken. Still, she *was* enjoying all the attention.

But why was Clint being so attentive to her? By the time he returned with her punch, she was in a state of high anxiety, torn between simply letting go and enjoying the evening or trying to find out the hard truth.

"Thank you." While she drank her punch she decided to forego her usual steamroller tactics and try for the subtle approach.

"You've been awfully kind to me lately," she said.

He laughed. "Are you searching for ulterior motives?"

"Perhaps. The fact is, I'm not accustomed to this kind of attention."

"It's their loss."

Clint tried for a light touch and bombed. Obviously she was searching for the truth, and who could blame her after the way they'd started off.

He didn't even know the truth himself, but one good thing about her not-so-subtle inquiry: it brought him to his senses. Actually, that wasn't the whole truth. It brought him *partially* to his senses.

It was hard to face a woman with shining eyes and flushed cheeks and still have all his cognitive abilities functioning full force.

Look at it this way, he told himself. *C. J. Maxey just saved your bachelor butt.*

"Clint, I want you to know how much all this means to me."

Here we go down the garden path. Careful, old boy, you'll lose your sense of direction.

Or indirection.

"I'm glad you're having fun," he said. "What's life if not fun?"

"I see the band coming back."

"Excuse me a minute."

He left her quickly because he couldn't stand to

see the disappointment in her face. Earlier in the evening she'd glowed with bright expectation, and he'd had a hard time keeping his hands off her. Several times he'd wanted to lean down and nuzzle her soft, dewy cheek. He'd wanted to capture her berry-colored lips in a kiss that had absolutely no regard for its audience. He'd come dangerously close to putting his lips close to her ear and whispering romantic nonsense.

"Saved by an uncompromising intelligence."

He was still muttering to himself when he reached the bandstand.

"What's up, Clint?"

"We're about to wind down here, Rick."

"Okay, the boys and I will play some romantic ballads." Rick winked. "Give you a good excuse to cuddle up with your girl."

"She's not my girl."

"Whatever you say."

"I don't want any slow music. Do the shake, rattle and roll stuff."

"Okay, but man, if it was me I'd seize every opportunity to get close. She's a classy chick."

"I'll tell her you said so." Clint shook hands all around. "Thanks for coming on such short notice. After I take her home, I'll meet you at Snookie's Den for beers."

"Man, you must be losing your touch."

"Yep. This tomcat's getting too old to howl."

He left them laughing, which was exactly his intent. No use inviting further questions. He'd never been one to discuss his business, and he wasn't about to lay himself open to speculation about why he had gone to such elaborate lengths for a woman he planned to take home and leave at her front door with nothing more than a kiss.

Maybe not even that. Maybe he'd just shake her hand.

The kiss took on a life of its own. Clint blamed it on the moon. He'd never seen such a spectacular sight, a giant golden orb suspended between a night-black sky and the quiet lake tucked onto the back of C.J.'s daddy's property.

He was the one who had suggested the drive with the top down. To cool off after the dance, he'd told her, and naturally she'd agreed. She was the one who suggested this made-for-lovers spot on her farm where stars were so close they seemed to be caught in her hair, on her skin and, most tempting of all, on her ever-so-slightly parted lips. "Will you look at that moon?" he said, turning off the ignition.

He didn't know exactly what happened after that. C.J. shifted to get a better view and she smelled sweet and she was only an arm's reach away. And suddenly...

This mind-blowing kiss that fanned fires he knew he'd never be able to control, no matter how hard he tried.

Why fight it?

He'd heard that voice before. It was probably the devil urging him on, throwing fresh kindling on flames that were blazing away on their own.

Maybe if he eased back a bit, maybe if he put her delectable breasts out of contact with his chest, he could still save both of them.

From the urgent sounds she was making, Lee County's dairy princess wasn't in any mood to be saved. She wanted to wallow in whatever he was offering. And the sooner the better.

Put that way, Clint decided the only gentlemanly thing to do would be to relieve her sexual distress. And his. If he didn't get some relief soon he was going to go crazy.

Fortunately her dress didn't have much of a top. Lots of skin, barely any material. He lowered his mouth to her long, slender throat and kissed her pulse point until her breath was hitching.

"Clint, please."

Ah, just what he wanted to hear. The soft pleas of a wanting woman.

Her bodice toppled like the walls of Jericho, and he zoomed in to claim the prize. His mouth closed over a dewy, rosy-tipped breast. Small and pert. Just right for a hungry man who hadn't even realized he'd been starving until he'd tasted the nectar.

She tangled her hands in his hair and pulled him closer. "That feels absolutely *wonderful*."

She made him feel like a hero. Cupping her face he kissed her and almost drowned in tenderness.

C.J. trembled. If that wasn't enough to give a man a big head, he didn't know what was. How many women could pull that innocent stuff off and make it seem real? Not many.

His fingertips brushed against silk, hot, damp silk that inflamed him. As if he needed any further prodding.

"You're wearing too many clothes, sweetheart."

He slipped the wisp of silk down her long, long

legs, and there happened to be enough moonlight so he could see she'd been wearing pink silk panties. Smaller ones this time, but pink, nonetheless.

Had she done it deliberately? Had she remembered how he'd loved seeing her in innocent pink silk?

Probably. His ego puffed up another notch. Pretty soon his head would be too big to fit into his motorcycle helmet.

Small price to pay for paradise. Dangerous thinking for a man determined to make this the kind of brief encounter that's pleasurable in the moonlight but forgotten as soon as the sun pinks the east.

He slid his fingers inside her, and she moaned and thrashed about as if he'd not only invented sex but won the Nobel Prize for his discovery. His desire ratcheted up another notch.

And so did the heat. "It's hot in this car."

"Hmm," she said, hardly sounding conscious.

"You don't mind if I take off my clothes, do you?"

"Hmm." Was that a yes or no? He'd take it for a yes, especially since she was helping him with the buttons.

His shirt went one way, his belt the other. It was when he kicked off his shoes and tried to divest himself of his tight slacks that he discovered the reason cars had steering wheels: to foil lovers.

He banged his knee, then his elbow, and next his head.

"Why couldn't somebody make these things collapsible?" he grumbled. "Or at the very least, removable?"

She made that sexy sound again halfway between a groan and a plea. It was doing wonders for his libido. He felt as if he'd been dumped in a vat of fault-less starch.

"Why don't we get in the back seat where we have more room?" She still wasn't talking, and so he opened the door on his side and sort of hopscotched around the car.

When he opened the door she tumbled out the way his laundry did after he'd overstuffed the closet. He caught her and proceeded, hero-like, to the back seat of his Corvette convertible.

Lord, he hadn't made out in the back seat of a car since he was a teenager. He couldn't blame that on the moon. He placed the blame squarely on the woman in his arms.

She must be a witch, otherwise why was he feeling like a sixteen-year-old about to get his first taste of paradise?

She looked lovely lying there with her breasts bare and her skirts tumbling around her like the petals of some exotic flower.

"You're so beautiful."

She whispered, "Thank you," then held up her slender arms, and he fell like Ulysses under enchant-ment. Her lips held the magic potion, and he feasted until he was drunk.

He wanted to taste every inch of her skin, to ex-plore every silky centimeter.

He started with her toes, nibbling until she was moaning, then slid his tongue back and forth over the length of her calf, then draped her leg over his shoul-der and addressed the sensitive skin at the back of her knee.

She was making gratifying sounds that spurred him to further feats of derring-do.

When the tip of his magic sword entered her, she jumped as if she'd been shot.

"Did I hurt you?"

"No. No." She reached for him, touched him, caressed him, and his secret weapon became blue steel. "Please, I want…this."

She'd given him plenty of reason to think so. But what an odd way to put it. Based on some of her earlier behavior, especially when she'd been wearing that hot red dress, he'd have expected C. J. Maxey to come forth with a little steamy sex talk at a time like this.

"So do I." He'd just become the master of understatement. You'd think a man who made his living with words could do better.

Considering the circumstances, though, the fact that his mind had imploded and his body was fixing to, he was lucky he could talk at all.

He kissed her until she was moaning again, and then delved into that sweet little honey pot she was suddenly trying to hide between clenched thighs. All his blood had departed his brain and gone south for the duration, otherwise he might have heard the alarm bells clanging.

Why didn't she loosen up? "C.J.?"

"Hmm."

"Could you relax a little bit? I won't bite."

"I know."

"Okay, then. Just…" He put one hand on her knee and parted her thighs. "Let me give us both some relief."

"Hmm."

He'd never seen eyes wider. Or more innocent-looking. A man could drown in eyes like that. As a matter of fact, he was drowning. He was going down, down…

"What the—?" Now he was the one jumping as if a squad of forty-four Magnums were firing at random.

"Clint…" She reached for him and he evaded her, which was a spectacular feat for a rather large naked man at full mast in the back seat of a very small car. Some might even say it was a miracle.

"Where are my damned pants?"

"Your pants?"

"Yes, madame. My pants."

It was hard to talk through gritted teeth. He figured he'd fractured at least one molar. Served him right for being such an idiot.

How could he not have known? All the signs were there.

"You don't want me?" she asked. Just like a little girl who'd been told she was uninvited to a birthday party.

Well, hell.

He stopped his frantic search for cover and kneaded the side of her cheek with his fist.

"It's not that I don't want you, sweetheart."

"You don't like virgins?"

"I don't know. I've never had one…and I don't intend for you to be the first."

"Oh…" She flushed so bright he could see it even though it was dark and the moon had scuttled behind a cloud. "This is so embarrassing." She pulled up her bodice and clutched it over her breasts like one of those old silent film stars in the movies he often watched late at night when he couldn't sleep.

"Nothing to be embarrassed about."

She unkinked her legs and smoothed down her skirt. "I feel so foolish. Naturally you expected a woman my age…" Her voice got a little hitch, and for a terrifying moment Clint thought she was going to cry.

Now that *would* be embarrassing. He was totally helpless in the face of a crying woman. She'd find out that Mr. Seen-it-all-done-it-all wasn't as tough as he'd seemed.

Fortunately for him, she pulled herself together. In fact she sat straight up in the back seat and announced, "I wish you'd put your clothes on."

How she could go from cringing to bossy in a split second boggled his mind…and cleared his senses.

"I should have known better than to bring you out here." He stomped around the car. Actually he *paraded,* but not before he'd postured and preened.

"*You're* the one who insisted on a drive," she said.

He jerked his pants on. One thing he could say about C.J.'s rage: it took the starch out of a man. "Well, *you're* the one who suggested a canoodle on your daddy's farm."

"I did *not* suggest we *canoodle.* I said, Let's look at the moon over the lake."

"Same damned thing."

"You have a one-track mind."

He buttoned his shirt crooked and had to start all over again. "I didn't hear you complaining."

"No. *You're* the one complaining."

"I wasn't complaining. I was merely pointing out the facts."

"That you don't do virgins."

"Damned straight."

"Ha." She flounced out of the back seat and slammed the door.

"What does that mean?"

"It means just what it sounds like. *Ha!*"

"You're the damnedest woman I've ever met." He put his belt on and climbed behind the wheel. The sooner he got out of this godforsaken town, the better.

Until then, he was going to keep his distance from C. J. Maxey, pageant or no pageant.

"What are you waiting for?" he said. "Get in the car."

"Gentlemen open car doors for ladies."

"Hell." He went around the car and jerked open her door. "Be my guest, your royal majesty."

"I wouldn't get in the car with you if you were the last man on earth."

"Well, you're sure as hell not going to walk. Get in the car, C.J."

"I *am* going to walk."

She struck out across the pasture with her nose lifted so high she'd drown if it started to rain. He thought about letting her go her stubborn way. After all, it was *her* farm. She'd know the way back home.

In the dark?

"Come back here," he roared.

"Make me."

That did it. He prided himself on his skill as a runner. Shoot, he'd run track in high school and college. Came close to setting a few records, then his mother died and all the competitive fire went out of him.

He'd have Miss C. J. Maxey cornered in no time flat. And then, heaven help her, that's all he could say.

"You asked for it."

He sprinted off and was gaining rapidly when a dastardly pothole jumped into his path and sent him sprawling. Clint crashed like a felled redwood.

That stopped the runaway princess. She turned, looked over her shoulder and came running back to him.

"Are you hurt?"

"Never better."

He hurt like hell, but he wouldn't have admitted it if eighteen elephants were stomping on his chest.

"Here," she said, offering her hand, "let me help you up."

"I don't need your assistance."

"Are you sure you're okay? You don't sound too good."

"That's my usual stud-bites-the-dust voice."

She laughed. Darn her pretty hide, she had to go and laugh, which spoiled his bad mood. When you thought about it, there was something pretty funny about a hundred-and-eighty-pound man sprawled in a cow pasture all because he'd been chasing a woman he had no business bringing out there in the first place.

Some would call it comeuppance.

"I guess you think that's pretty funny, huh?"

"Yes." She could hardly speak between great wheezes of laughter.

"Maybe you'll think this is even funnier."

Clint grabbed her hand and tugged her down right on top of him. Then they both laughed so hard they had to hang on to each other. And he'd guarantee *that* proximity was going nowhere, not after the lesson he'd learned.

"Oh, my." She wiped her eyes. "What a way to end an evening."

"Laughter's the best medicine." He grinned. "I made that up."

"It's the most original thought I've ever heard."

She was laughing again, great peals of full-bodied mirth with her head thrown back and her slender neck bared to the moon. Just right for kissing. If you were dumb enough to make the same mistake twice.

"As much as I enjoy sitting in this cow pasture with a frustrated, angry princess on my knee, I think it's time to go home. What do you say?"

"I say, what took you so long? A girl could fall in a pothole out here and break her neck."

Chapter Sixteen

"Ellie, you're wearing a dress!"

"Don't you think it's high time? Most folks around here don't even know I have legs."

Ellie stood on C.J.'s front porch for the first time since she'd left. It wasn't the dress that stood out, though, it was Ellie herself. She positively glowed.

C.J. didn't have to guess the reason. She heard him coming down the hall saying, "Is that Ellie?"

"Yes, Dad, it's Ellie."

"Well, well." He took both Ellie's hands. "Don't you look gorgeous!"

"You make me feel young and beautiful."

"You *are*."

What Sam did next astonished C.J., though having seen the same behavior when her mother was alive, she shouldn't have been surprised. He kissed Ellie softly on the mouth, then whirled her around the front porch in an impromptu waltz as if a twenty-piece orchestra were playing in three-four time.

The thing that surprised C.J. was the jealousy she felt. It was merely a twinge, but still it was there. Oh, she wasn't afraid of being usurped in her father's affections. Nothing like that. And she was very happy for them, truly she was. But still she couldn't help recall the recent debacle in the cow pasture. Though both she and Clint had laughed the whole thing off, which was about the best you could ask for under the circumstances, still C.J. felt that some important connection had been broken.

He didn't call anymore, didn't drop by. Though he was supposed to cover the state pageant, she had no idea whether he'd be there.

"Are you ready to go, C.J.?" Ellie was looking at her with a wise and knowing expression.

Don't say anything, C.J. silently pleaded, and Ellie picked up her signals.

"As ready as I'll ever be," she said.

"I'll load the bags." Sam trotted off whistling, and after he'd stowed her bags he kissed C.J. on the cheek. "Knock 'em dead this week, sweetheart. Sandi and I will be down Friday to see you in the finals."

C.J. didn't say, "I probably won't make the finals." She simply said, "Okay, Dad. Have a good week. We'll see you Friday."

The minute they got in the car, Ellie asked, "What was that all about back there on the porch?"

"Nothing I can talk about right now."

"Fine. If you want to talk, just let me know."

"Let's talk about you and Dad."

Ellie grinned. "I hope you're as happy with developments as I am."

"Nothing could make me happier than to see you and Dad married."

"Sam's not ready for that. I don't know if he ever will be."

"Oh, I think he will."

Ellie glanced at her, then changed the subject. "It's a long ride to Jackson, C.J. Plenty of time for you to back out if you don't want to do this."

"I've come this far. I might as well go all the way...for once in my life."

"That's a strange way of putting it."

"It has been a strange summer."

"Strange but wonderful." Ellie turned onto the Natchez Trace Parkway and cruised toward the site of the long-awaited state dairy princess pageant.

"What's the matter with your leg?"

Clint had been sitting at his desk waiting for Wayne to come along and ask that question. "Took a little tumble." He said it offhand as if he'd spilled down the steps drunk instead of landing in a hole while making a total jerk of himself over C.J.

"My trick ankle went out."

"You need all that for a sprained ankle?"

Wayne surveyed the thick Ace bandage, the crutches leaning against the desk, the footstool Clint had propped his foot on.

"With this type of injury, you can't be too careful."

Wayne rubbed the beard stubble which Clint suspected he kept for exactly that purpose. Nothing more dramatically portrays puzzlement than a thinking man worrying two-day-old beard stubble.

"I seem to recall this is the first day of the state's dairy princess competition." Clint decided to let that remark ride. "I guess you're going to tell me the trick ankle is why you're not there."

"I figured it would hamper my ability to move around and get the stories. I figured you'd send Charlie while I stayed here to cover sports."

Wayne laughed until tears rolled down his cheeks. Even though it was at his expense, Clint endured his boss's bout of hilarity with good grace. He was an easygoing man. He could take whatever Wayne dished out…as long as he didn't send him to Jackson.

Clint didn't relish the idea of facing C. J. Maxey again. Not that he was cowardly, mind you. He knew an exit scene when he saw one. Not only had he seen it, he'd been the star.

"The good citizens of Hot Coffee would laugh me out of business if I let you cover sports."

"I admit to a few shortcomings in that department, but I'm not that bad."

"On the other hand, can you imagine what Charlie would write about the princesses? 'Eighty-two pretty gals squared off against each other on the playing field.'"

"That's not bad."

"I want heart. I want soul. I want drama." Wayne punctuated each sentence with a right jab in the air.

"We're wading knee deep in it right now."

"I want you to ditch the props and get down there as fast as you can, otherwise you're going to see some real drama."

"Murder?"

"Mayhem for starters. I can always advance to the big leagues."

"You're a hard man."

"Yep. Now get your posterior out of that chair and on the road."

"Posterior?"

"I run a family paper around here."

Clint unwrapped the bandage and flung it onto his desk, then tossed his crutches. "Hey, Wayne, catch."

Wayne chuckled. "Have fun."

"I intend to."

And he did. If he had to go, he might as well make the most of the situation. Look at it this way, he told himself. He'd be surrounded by a bevy of beauties. There ought to be at least one who'd take his mind off C.J.

Eighty-one other girls attended an exercise in tedium called *orientation,* and every one of them beautiful. C.J. felt like a toad among lilies.

Gathered in a classroom on Millsaps College campus, the young women vying for the title of Mississippi Dairy Princess looked as if they'd been grooming for the title all their lives. With rapt faces turned toward Leroy Levant, the pageant's director, they nodded and smiled and scribbled on little pink notepads.

If the judges were spying from the wings looking for imposters, C.J. had already lost the pageant. She was not only *not* taking notes, she was having a hard time to keep from laughing.

"The young woman who represents the dairy industry of the greeeat state of Mississippi—'' Leroy paused for an explosion of applause ''—must be above, I say *above,* reproach. No smoking, no drinking, no sneaking out of the dorm after lights…no matter how good-looking your boyfriend is.'' Another pause for the giggles that swept the audience.

''Naturally, the big stuff is forbidden. Marriage, pregnancy, felony convictions, any unethical behavior of any sort… You haven't posed for *Playboy,* have you?''

Leroy's question was a direct reference to the scandal that had swept the pageant in 1995. The top contender was disqualified when he'd discovered that she was Miss December for a magazine that required she wear nothing but a red hat with a pompom on the end.

Nobody was going to ask C.J. to be Miss December.

She glanced around the audience searching for a certain tall man with black hair, blue eyes and devilment in his soul. Not that she wanted to see him. Far from it. She wanted to spot Clint Garrett so she could avoid him.

Up front Leroy Levant finished his spiel with, ''Our celebrity master of ceremonies will be none other than movie star Dolly Wilder.''

Afterward they had social hour, which turned out to be girls dividing into clusters around three punch bowls and ten sheet cakes shaped like the state of Mississippi and iced with black and white to represent Holstein cows.

Left to her own devices, C.J. wandered among them listening to snatches of conversation and searching for a name tag that read Gabrielle Jones. Her roommate.

She didn't find Gabrielle, but she did find Clint Garrett.

"Oh, just look at what walked in." The girl gushing over the late arrival looked like Alice in Wonderland complete with flaxen hair and wide blue eyes.

All the girls craned their necks toward the door, and there he stood bigger than life, the bane of C.J.'s existence, the man who drove her crazy with desire and mad with frustration. Hot Coffee's ace reporter in black leather with his helmet dangling from his hand.

"He looks just like Tom Cruise," the Alice lookalike said and the brunette next to her giggled.

"Except taller."

"Yeah. At least a foot."

Spotting his enraptured admirers, Clint lifted an eyebrow. C.J. wanted to clobber him. The rake. The cad. The virgin hater.

She spun around so she wouldn't have to look. Furthermore she certainly didn't want him spotting her.

"Somebody you know?" C.J. nearly bumped into the girl who'd asked the question. "Hi, I'm Gabrielle Jones." She laughed. "I always get that reaction. French mother, American-as-apple-pie father... Call me Gabby."

"C. J. Maxey." C.J. took the extended hand and was surprised to encounter a solid, no-nonsense grip. "Yes, I know him."

"But wish you didn't?"

"Something like that."

If Gabby pursued the subject, C.J. was going to request another roommate.

"Well, C. J. Maxey, since we're going to be roommates, why don't we find a quiet spot somewhere so we can get better acquainted?"

"Perfect. Someplace out of here?"

"My thoughts exactly. I know a great hamburger joint."

"Good. I'm starving."

C.J. could *feel* him back there emitting sexual currents, probably trying to reel in one of the raving beauties who wouldn't be burdened down with an unfortunate case of virginity.

"Let's get out of here," she said.

The flaming redhead with the devil-may-care attitude was the woman Clint would have picked to take his mind off his troubles, but she had one fatal flaw. She was in the company of C. J. Maxey.

He searched the room for another possibility, but out of the corner of his eye he saw C.J. and the redhead leaving. Now where in the devil were they going and why?

How could a man concentrate on charming a comely miss when C.J. was loose on the town doing no telling what?

He needed some fresh air. Maybe he'd take his Harley down to the Ross Barnett reservoir. Maybe peace and quiet was what he needed.

As he hurried out the door he caught a glimpse of long, trim legs and dark feathery hair.

Maybe he'd just mosey down the street and see what C.J. was up to. Given her penchant for getting into trouble, she was liable to need his help.

Chapter Seventeen

C.J. had learned stress eating from Ellie. If she got as big as a house, that's who she'd blame.

Here she was sitting in a corner booth consuming a triple scoop milkshake featuring three kinds of ice cream, a double-decker hamburger with all the trimmings and a platter of fried onion rings on the side. And all because Clint was crammed up against her pressing his leg against her thigh—*deliberately,* she had no doubt—while he pretended to be interviewing Gabby.

She and her roommate had been having a nice getting-to-know-you conversation when all of a sudden he'd horned in and had completely taken over.

C.J. was speechless with rage and overactive hormones. Across the table, her roommate didn't seem to be having the same trouble. She toyed with a diet cola while she told Clint how her life's ambition was to be Mississippi's Dairy Princess.

She wasn't kidding, either. Any fool could see that. In the face of all that sincerity, C.J. felt like a great, big fraud.

"I grew up in the dairy industry," Gabby was saying. "I've been coming to the pageants since I was three years old. Daddy would always say, 'Someday you'll be wearing the crown, Gabby, and that'll be the proudest day of my life.'"

"He must be very proud of you, then."

Oh, Clint was smooth the way he got his story while posing as a woman's best friend. The next thing she knew, he'd be hustling Gabby off to the reservoir with a fishing pole, encouraging her to go swimming in her birthday suit.

C.J. tried to drown the green-eyed monster with milkshake, but it didn't work. He kept poking and prodding until the only thing she could do was excuse herself and go off to the bathroom where she could kick the stall door and pretend it was Clint.

She was fixing to do just that when Gabby said, "I'm sure he would have been. Dad was killed in a freak accident on the dairy farm ten years ago."

Now C.J. felt about two inches tall. She felt like something that ought to be squashed under somebody's foot.

"I'm so sorry," she said, meaning she was not only sorry for Gabby's loss but sorry for reacting like a jealous teenager instead of a sane and compassionate adult.

Nobody paid her any attention, but she stayed anyway. She was completely out of the mood to kick doors, especially after Clint said, "I suppose your mother's here to watch," and Gabby told him, "No. We couldn't afford for Mom to come. But she's keeping her fingers crossed.

"Please don't print that," she added. "I don't want sympathy support because of a sob story."

"You have my word of honor," Clint said.

C.J. couldn't even be miffed about that. He *was* a man of honor, otherwise he'd have taken full advantage of her on more occasions than she cared to remember, especially on the night she had too many green monkeys.

"Thank you," Gabby said. "I'm here because I want to help promote the dairy industry my father devoted his life to."

And I'm here under false pretenses.

All too aware of the heart-wrenching story unfolding across the table and Clint's body heat, C.J. attacked her onion rings as if they were going to fight back. Suddenly there was a lull in the conversation and she looked up to see Clint staring at her.

"That looks delicious," he said, and although she knew darned good and well he was talking about onion rings, all she could think about was the two of them tangled together in the back seat of his Corvette.

"It is." She licked her bottom lip. "I'll give you some."

"You will?"

His tone of voice, his body language, his eyes...everything about him shouted *sex*. The air between them sizzled. It's a wonder Gabby didn't feel the heat.

"Anytime," C.J. said.

"I think I'll help myself, then."

"Why don't you do just that?"

"You're sure you won't mind?"

"On the contrary. I'd be delighted."

"Good."

Without taking his eyes off her, Clint reached into the plate and nabbed an onion ring. The way he savored it ought to be X-rated. She watched, drooling, but who cared? She'd made a fool of herself over him so many times, what did one more matter?

Gabby cleared her throat. "If you guys will excuse me, I'll head on back to the dormitory. I promised Mom I'd give her a call."

C.J. roused from her steamy stupor long enough to say, "See you later, Gabby."

Then she was left all alone with Clint. Not really, of course, because the restaurant was crowded, but that's how she felt.

Just how she'd gone from fury to frenzy was a mystery to her, but she was too busy panting to figure it out.

Clint lifted another onion ring off the plate. "Open wide, C.J."

She bit down, and he leaned over and took the other end in his mouth. When their lips met in the middle, he made no bones about his motives...or hers. Clint Garrett was out to kiss her, and she was out to let him.

There's something exciting and rewarding about kissing in public. It makes a woman feel as if she's been claimed by her special man. A public kiss shouts, "Hands off, everybody: she's mine."

C.J. closed her eyes and murmured, "Hmm," not caring who saw or heard.

"You like that, do you?"

"There's more where that came from."

"Good. I'm greedy. I want it all."

They ate the rest of her food the same way, including the hamburger. By the time they'd finished it was dark.

"I'll walk you back to your dormitory."

Outside he slid an arm around her waist and she fell into step beside him.

"Does this mean we're becoming friends, C.J.?"

"It looks that way."

"It feels that way."

"Yes, it does."

"Beats fighting."

"I agree."

"Though I'll have to admit that the last fight we had was a lot of fun."

"You enjoy falling?"

"Yes, as long as you're on top."

All sorts of erotic images spun through C.J.'s mind, and she played the game she'd played a dozen times since that ill-fated night. What if she had made love with Clint? Would she have been a one-night stand, or would they still be sharing a bed? What if he hadn't pulled back at the last minute? Would it have been merely sex or something more?

What if they'd fallen in love?

"Are you thinking about the pageant, C.J.?"

"No."

"Neither am I."

"The dorm's just up ahead," she said.

He pulled her off the sidewalk and into the deep shadows of an enormous magnolia tree, and there he kissed her with an intensity that seared her soul.

I'm falling in love, she thought. He pulled her closer and deepened the kiss and she thought, *I am in love.*

Heaven help her, C. J. Maxey had fallen for the wrong man. Oh, he had his good qualities. In fact, he had many wonderful qualities—lively wit, a great sense of humor, an old-fashioned streak of honor, intelligence, kindness. The list could go on and on, but the bottom line was, Clint was not the marrying kind.

He might as well have *traveling man* tattooed on his forehead. He'd made it perfectly clear he didn't have roots and didn't want any.

What was she going to do?

"I like you, C. J. Maxey."

A beam of moonlight found its way through the branches and fell across his face, and she gazed at him, blinded by blue eyes and love.

"As crazy as it seems, I like you, too."

"I hope you win this pageant and all your dreams come true."

She didn't want to win. Not anymore. Not after seeing girls like Gabby to whom the title and the scholarship money would mean so much.

But saying so would have been ungracious, so she merely said, "Thank you."

"You're a rare woman, C.J. You deserve the very best of everything. You deserve a great life and a great man, somebody worthy of you."

"Clint…"

He put a finger over her lips. "I'll be around all

week. If you need anything, give a yell and I'll come running." His smile was bittersweet. "Just like a regular hero."

"This sounds like goodbye."

"It is. After this week, I'm leaving."

Her heart tried to pound its way out of her chest. She couldn't breathe, couldn't think.

"Where are you going?"

"Someplace different."

Someplace where she wasn't. All her instincts screamed that she was right.

"Is it because of me?"

"No."

Was he lying? Or was she fooling herself about her importance to him?

She would probably never know.

"I wish you all the luck in the world," she said, and he looked at her as if he'd expected more.

But what more could she say? She had nothing to guide her except a few mind-boggling kisses. No pretty words, no promises, nothing.

The silence between them stretched for eons, while C.J. replayed every encounter she'd had with him. They'd shot sparks off each other from the very beginning. Being together had never been easy for them, but it had never been dull.

And she was going to miss him terribly.

"Clint Garrett, you're the best time I ever had."

He lifted an eyebrow and gave her the cocky smile she'd loved so well. "That goes for me, too, C. J. Maxey. You're still the damnedest woman I ever met."

"I'll take that as a compliment."

"That's the way I meant it."

They got lost in another deep silence. Sexual currents zinged between them, and C.J. wondered if he felt the same tugging on his heartstrings that she did. Probably not. If so, why was he saying goodbye? Why was he leaving town?

"Well…" she said, hoping he'd say, "I've changed my mind. I was just testing you to see how you felt about me. I'm not really going to leave. *I love you.*"

Foolish fancies. Of course he wasn't going to say any of those things. After all, he was who he was, and she was who she was.

Still, she had to touch him. One more time.

She put her hand on his broad chest, right over his heart. "Take care of yourself," she whispered.

"You, too." He covered her hand with his, ever so tenderly, ever so briefly.

And then he vanished into the night. Quickly. Before she could look into his eyes and see his soul.

Chapter Eighteen

That was a first for Clint—saying goodbye, telling a woman his plan. The only excuse he could make was that C.J. wasn't just any woman. She was a rare combination of wit and intelligence, the kind of woman he'd have fallen for if he were the falling kind.

Sitting in the back of the auditorium watching the contestants rehearse for Friday night's events, he amused himself thinking of ways he could help C.J. win.

Just look at her. Poised, classy, winsome. She deserved to win.

And he was going to do everything he could to help her cause. Not that she needed his help. Scuttlebutt had it that C. J. Maxey was taking the pageant by storm. Seems the judges had taken a liking to her refreshing honesty and her wholesome good looks.

* * *

The newspapers splashed C.J. all over the head-lines, touting her as the clear front-runner in this year's hotly contested dairy princess pageant.

C.J. glanced at the byline. Wouldn't you know? Clint Garrett. He made her sound like a cross between Greta Garbo (all that mystery) and Gwyneth Paltrow (all that class).

She would have been flattered and somewhat amused if it weren't for Gabby. C.J. glanced at the other twin bed where her roommate sat reading the same evening edition of the newspaper.

Gabby looked up and smiled. "Congratulations, C.J. It couldn't happen to a nicer person."

"This is all speculative."

"I don't think so. Everybody was talking about how well you did in the preliminary interviews."

"I heard the same thing about you." It was true. Alice in Wonderland had been green with envy. So had Senator Crumb's daughter, who was the only other woman in the pageant as plain as C.J.

"Oh, well..." Gabby waved the encouragement away. "I have lots more years to enter, and this is your last chance. I really hope you win, C.J."

C.J. flung the newspaper onto the bedside table and grabbed her jeans and T-shirt. "Don't count yourself out, Gabby. It's not over till it's over."

"You're not leaving?"

"Yes."

"But it's after curfew. If they catch you, you'll be disqualified."

Wouldn't that be a good thing? It would solve at least half of C.J.'s problems.

"I'll take my chances."

"Be careful, C.J."

"If I see Leroy Levant, I promise I'll run the other way."

"Who wouldn't?"

C.J. opened the door a crack to reconnoiter the hall, then slipped out and down the stairs. Five flights. Echoing with emptiness.

Outside she hailed a cab. "The Marriott, please." She hadn't called ahead. Maybe the element of surprise would be in her favor.

Slipping through the lobby she kept an eye out for Leroy Levant or one of the judges. Not that she minded getting thrown out of the pageant. But not yet. Not until she talked with Ellie.

She knocked on the door of the Magnolia Suite, and Ellie's old college chum, Dolly Wilder, opened the door. C.J. hadn't counted on this.

"Miss Wilder, when did you get in?"

"I breezed in this afternoon...on my broom, that witch with the *Hollywood Tattler* would say." She opened the door wide. "Come in. Ellie's in the bathroom. C.J.? Right?"

"Yes, Miss Wilder."

"Good heavens. I taught you your first dirty word. You were two years old and mad as a hornet, and I said, 'Just stomp your feet and say *dammit,* C.J. It'll make you feel better,' and you did. Lord, Phoebe wanted to strangle me."

The fiftyish star of film and stage, who could have passed for thirty-five even in strong sunlight, gave a full-throated laugh and the just-between-us wink that was her trademark onstage and off.

"Call me Dolly." She pulled C.J. inside. "Let me look at you. You have Phoebe's eyes. She had the most incredible eyes. All she had to do was *look* at a man, and he was smitten."

Dolly Wilder had some amazing eyes herself. C.J. had never seen eyes that color. Amber. Her hair was loose and long, a pale blond color that probably came from a bottle but looked natural. Even in a pair of black sweats faded almost gray she was one of the most beautiful women C.J. had ever seen.

She vaguely remembered Dolly flitting in and out of their house during her childhood, but then she'd become a superstar and C.J. didn't see her again until Phoebe's funeral.

"I'm having a glass of wine. Can I pour you a drink?"

"No, you may not." Ellie came out of the bathroom in her chenille robe. "You taught her enough bad habits."

"How do you know?"

"I was there when you taught her to swear. Remember?"

"Damn. I don't have any secrets from you."

"No, you don't." Ellie nabbed a glass of wine and made herself comfortable on the sofa. "You're breaking curfew, C.J. This must be important."

"It is."

Now that she was here, C.J. couldn't bring herself to tell Ellie why she'd come.

"You must be feeling pretty good," Ellie told her. "I hear you're the front-runner."

"I think that's mostly in Clint Garrett's imagination."

"No," Dolly said. "It's true. The judges call you a 'breath of fresh air.' I think they appreciate your honesty."

"I don't feel honest. I feel like a fraud. I *am* a fraud."

Ellie patted the sofa. "Come over here and sit down and tell me all about it."

It felt good to have the comfort of a warm and motherly embrace. C.J. basked in the warmth while she gathered her courage.

"I don't want to disappoint you, Ellie, or to cause you or Dad or my hometown any embarrassment, but I'd like to withdraw from the pageant."

Ellie nodded as if that was what she'd expected to hear all along. "You won't disappoint or embarrass anybody, so put that out of your mind and do what is best for *you*. What made you change your mind?"

"A lot of things. My roommate, for one. This pageant and the scholarship money mean *everything* to her. If I pull out I think she has a shot at the title."

"The scholarship money would mean a lot to you."

"You know, I've always said I couldn't go to vet school because of Dad and finances, but that was a crutch. Dad's more than capable of taking care of himself, and I've always had the power to leave here and do what I please. I've just never had the courage."

"Sometimes it takes us a while to see the truth, especially if it's about ourselves. Some people never do."

"Now that Dad has you…"

"Not yet, but I'm working on it."

"With a little help from me," Dolly chimed in. "Lord, how I love fixing other people's problems."

A look passed between them, then Ellie and her old college chum lifted their glasses and said, "To the Foxes. Long may we howl."

"And prowl," Dolly added.

"Hear, hear."

"If I had a glass I could toast, too," C.J. said.

"Oh, hell. Why not?"

Ellie poured C.J. a glass, but it was only half full, which was probably a very good thing considering she had no head for spirits of any kind.

She lifted her glass to theirs and took a long swig. Shoot, at the rate she was going—breaking curfews and no-drinking bans both—she wouldn't have to withdraw from the pageant: she'd be kicked out.

Wouldn't that make headlines?

"So, what are you going to do about your schooling?" Ellie asked.

"I'll get a student loan."

"Or apply for a scholarship," Dolly said.

"Yes, if I qualify for any."

"I've established scholarships all over the country. I'm thinking about setting one up for veterinary students." Seeing that C.J. was fixing to refuse, Dolly added, "Call it payback for a favor your mother did me a long time ago. Now tell me, where would you like to go?"

"Mississippi State."

"Done."

C.J. finished her wine, and Ellie offered to take her back to the dorm, but she said, "No, thanks."

She was twenty-five years old. It was high time for

her to stand on her hind legs, as the old saying goes, and take care of herself.

When she left she heard Dolly telling Ellie, "I used *this* with the Count. All I have to do is crook my little finger, and he comes running."

For a heady moment, C.J. imagined herself using a mysterious *something* that would have Clint Garrett at her beck and call, then she decided any attempt to enchant him would be perfectly useless. He was not the kind of man who would be any woman's slave. Ever.

The problem with having too much time on your hands is that you're likely to get into trouble. Big trouble.

That's exactly what had happened to Clint. There he'd been this afternoon, standing around backstage not bothering a soul, just thinking his own thoughts and trying not to be bored to death, when he'd overheard a conversation that could change the course of his life.

In the span of one afternoon he'd transformed from a man with nothing on his mind except doing the least amount of work possible to a man with a mission. He was onto a story, a very big story if his *source* and his instincts were right. He didn't yet know about the reliability of his source, but his instincts were seldom wrong.

The only problem was, he'd squelched them for so long, he was having to feel his way back to trust.

"Is that all?" His source was hidden in the shadows of the tall camellias. Nothing was visible except a small pale face.

Senator Tobias's daughter was terrified. Clint reached for her cold hands. "That's all for now. I'll let you know if I need anything else."

"I...you won't use my name?"

"No. Trust me. Reporters have gone to jail rather than reveal the identity of a source."

"I probably shouldn't have told you." She gave a nervous giggle. "But revenge is so sweet." She'd told Clint how her daddy forced her to end an affair with the only man she'd ever love.

The lights of a taxi illuminated the street, barely missing her hiding place.

"I'd better go."

"Yes. Be careful."

She scuttled out of the bushes and through the side door just as the taxi spit out its passenger, a tall woman listing dangerously to the left, a slender woman with a cap of feathery curls and an all-too-familiar laugh.

"No, thanks," she was saying. "I can see my way to the door."

Clint wanted to go out and smack the cab driver. He'd just bet the man wanted to accompany Miss C. J. Maxey to her door. He'd just bet the man wanted to play the gallant hero in return for a kiss or two. Or maybe more.

Roaring toward the cab like a bull turned loose on a matador, Clint grabbed C.J.'s arm—in the nick of time, he noted, for she leaned against him in a manner that had him wanting to steal a kiss or eight. Shoot. Eight wouldn't begin to be enough. Try a million.

"You've been drinking," he said, and when she turned a radiant smile on him he forgot everything except the feel of her slender arm beneath his fingers and the scent of jasmine that wafted off her hair.

"Just a little." A hiccup exploded and she covered her mouth. "That wasn't me."

"I know." He half dragged, half carried her to the camellia bushes, only this time he vanished into the shadows, too. "What are you trying to do? Get yourself thrown out of the pageant?"

She giggled. "Old Leroy would make me a legend. I'd be that wild, wanton woman caught drinking and consorting."

"Well, hell."

"Hell, hell, hell." She giggled. "The legend grows. Caught cussing, too. I think I'll yell it."

He clapped his hand over her mouth. C.J. was worse off than he'd first thought. She might as well just walk through the front door and give herself up as try to sneak. In her condition, C.J. *sneaking* was as ludicrous as a herd of elephants tiptoeing.

"I'm going to help you get back to your room."

She shook her head. "Mft nnnt gaaaa."

"If I take my hand off your mouth, will you behave?" She nodded her head, which probably didn't mean a thing. A woman like C.J. usually did exactly as she pleased. Damn the torpedoes and full speed ahead.

"Promise, now. Quiet." Clint removed his hand, and she shook her head like a puppy drunk on his first scent of clover. "I'll help you get back to your room, and if you're *very* quiet and do exactly as I say, I think we can make it without being discovered."

"I don't care. I don't want to be princess."

"You're serious, aren't you?"

"Yes."

"So you went out and had…how much wine? Two sips?" He remembered how drunk she'd become on one green monkey. C. J. Maxey was going to give him ulcers and premature baldness, besides. Not to mention the worst insomnia in the history of sleep disorders.

"Good lord, women like you shouldn't be allowed out of the house after dark without a chaperone."

His mind, already crowded with plots and subplots whirling around the dairy industry, tried to wrap itself around the latest problem with C.J. She was intent on getting kicked out of the pageant on grounds of drinking and carousing. Her daddy would be humiliated. Ellie would be mortified. The whole town would turn against her.

Clint had to do something.

A plan leaped into his mind, so beautiful in its simplicity that he wondered why he hadn't thought of it earlier.

"Here's what we're going to do. I'm taking you with me."

"Okeydokey." She plastered herself around him, and what could a man do but try to think pure thoughts? They didn't do him any good, but he tried anyway.

"We still have enough time to get the license."

"License? Are we going fishing?"

"No, we're going to get married."

Chapter Nineteen

C.J. couldn't make sense of anything after Clint said he was taking her with him except the wild beating of her heart and the wing-rustling of her lost hopes taking flight. And when he picked her up and carried her off into the night, she thought he looked exactly like Clark Cable carrying Vivian Leigh up the red-carpeted staircase to the bedroom that had been locked against him for so long.

And we all know where that leads.

Oh, she was a happy woman. A great song was in order. Something along the lines of "Wonderful Tonight." She opened her mouth to belt out Eric Clapton's hit, but Clint stopped her with a kiss that lasted a long, delicious time.

"I couldn't use my hands. They're full," he said after he broke it off.

"Goody. I love being your handful."

She wiggled her bottom to show how much she loved it, and he growled.

"You sound like a marauding lion."

"Close." He picked up his pace as if he were trying to outrun someone. "We're almost there."

"Okeydokey."

She wished she could think of something clever to say, something sexy, but she was wrapped in a warm, fuzzy blanket of wine, barely-hold-her-eyes-open fatigue and best-in-the-world arms.

"I'm going to have to put you down so I can get my key." He propped her against the wall so that she had a view of the full moon reflected in the swimming pool.

"Let's skinny-dip." She stripped off her T-shirt, and he said a word that curled her ears, then hustled her into his motel room.

"Damn it, C.J. Behave."

He jerked the bedspread off then picked her up and tossed her into the middle of the bed. "Sleep. We'll talk in the morning."

"Which side?"

"What do you mean, which side?"

Why was he acting so dense? Bringing her to his motel room had been his idea. If he kept this up, she was going to get good and mad at him.

"I sleep on the right side of the bed, but if that's the side you prefer I'm perfectly willing to concede."

He muttered a word she'd never heard except in movies, which just showed what an overprotected, naive person she was. She let loose a volley of hellfire-and-damnations just for the heady sense of release.

Clint stomped off toward the bathroom, and C.J. stripped off her clothes and waited under the sheets, breathless with nerves and desire.

Oh, she couldn't wait to lose her accursed virginity.

Thank God she was asleep. Or she could be faking it. With C.J. you never could tell.

Employing stealth and cunning to undress, Clint rolled into the discarded bedspread on the floor that was much more uncomfortable than he'd imagined. Didn't they put padding under the carpets in these cheap motel rooms? Didn't they ever vacuum?

Musty scents of ground-in dirt and long-ago exhaled cigarette smoke wafted up from the carpet. He was going to smother. He needed air.

Dragging the bedspread behind him, he tiptoed toward the door and banged his shin on a chair that leaped at him out of the dark. Clint bit back an oath, then glanced at the bed. C.J. hadn't moved.

Good. She was out cold.

He eased open the door then stuck his nose to the crack.

"Ahh," he said, then nearly choked on somebody else's cigarette smoke.

Clint felt beleaguered, insulted and put-upon. A suffering man is in no condition to sleep on the floor. He made his decision quickly, then climbed into bed beside C.J. before he could talk himself out of it.

He'd sleep on top of the covers. He'd stay *way* over on his side of the bed. He wouldn't move. He'd get up early and she'd never know.

It was a very good plan that might have worked if she hadn't inched across the great divide in the mid-

dle of the night and plastered herself all over him. It
still could have worked if she hadn't been naked and
he hadn't been aroused beyond the point of no return.
Even then it could have worked if she hadn't started
nibbling his neck and fondling his body and making
soft, sexy sounds that drove him berserk.

"C.J."

"Hmm?"

"Are you awake?"

"Uh-huh."

She continued her erotic explorations while he lay
there rigid, *rigid* being the operative word. He still
had a number of options. He could leap off the bed
and spend the rest of the night tortured by the floor
and regret. He could say, "Wait a minute. You're a
virgin, and I'm not a spoiler."

"Clint?" She tickled his ear with her whisper, and
then with her tongue.

"What?"

"I'm naked."

"I know."

How well he knew. Every nerve in his body
twanged. He was C. J. Maxey's musical instrument.
If she wanted to, she could sing country and western
songs to his ragged rhythm.

Still, if he bolted right now he might save them.

Then he made two fatal mistakes: he rolled over
and reached for her.

His intentions were good. He was going to hold her
shoulders, move her back to her side of the bed and
say, Go back to sleep. Instead he found himself in
full frontal contact with a determined, amorous

woman. Not just any amorous woman, mind you, but the one woman in the world he couldn't do without.

"I want you," she said, and although he knew he should say, No, he was in no condition to force the issue. Furthermore, he'd proposed and she'd said, Yes, so why not go ahead and have the honeymoon before the wedding? What was so bad about that?

Nothing that he could think of. But then, at the moment thinking was not his strong suit.

"Are you sure?" He had to ask the question, and when she said, "Yes," he figured he was the world's biggest fool if he didn't give them both some release.

Ever mindful of her innocence, he said, "I'll be gentle."

Starting with her shoulders he caressed the long, long length of her body, which turned out to be the most spectacular body he'd ever had his hands on. By the time he got down to her toes he felt like a bull elephant straining at a silk tether.

"Oh," she said, and that was all, but it was enough to spur him on. With lips and tongue, he started an erotic journey upward. If there had ever been anything more delectable than her soft skin, he didn't know what it was.

By the time he reached her thighs, she was liquid fire and he was lost. He dipped his tongue into the sweet hot center of her, and she tangled her hands in his hair and held him there for a small eternity.

He'd read somewhere that you know your special woman by the way she tastes. Finally, he'd discovered the truth.

Caught up in magic, he savored this new discovery while C.J. writhed beneath him making wanting sounds. She was no shy miss awaiting her sexual initiation with fear and trembling. No, indeed. She was a volcano waiting to erupt. She was a lusty woman getting ready to box his ears if he didn't give her what she craved.

Arching upward on the wave of an explosion, she screamed, "Now, Clint. Now."

She was the spurs to his stallion. Heady stuff, being the object of such desire. Still, in spite of her obvious eagerness, he'd be careful. He'd be gentle and easy. He'd hold back till she could adjust.

But C.J. was having none of that. When he entered her, she arched strongly against him and he was impaled.

He was enthralled. He was enchanted. He was in heaven.

"Oh, my," she whispered, and he said, "Oh, yes."

Now she was the one straining at silken cords, and he was the one holding back. If he moved right now, he'd spoil her pleasure.

"Shh. Be still. For just a minute."

He held her close so she couldn't move and stopped her questions with a kiss. A long kiss that lasted through the easy rhythm that finally started of its own accord.

He was telling himself to hold on and hold back when his untutored student tore off on an erotic gallop that had him panting and her screaming.

"Yes, yes, *yes!*"

She chanted her new mantra more than once, and Clint finally got the message: this was an initiation, not a taming. None of this gentle guidance through

the first steps for her. Nosirree. C. J. Maxey wanted
the whole nine yards.

In fact, she said so. "I want *everything,*" she said.

It would have been ungallant not to fulfill a lady's
request, especially a lady of such amazing natural ap-
titude that he'd left this earth and was romping
through paradise. He didn't plan on returning for a
very long time.

And he didn't.

Finally they fell against each other, sweat-slick and
sated. Clint rolled onto his back, taking her with him,
then fell asleep wearing a Cheshire cat's grin and C.
J. Maxey.

C.J. tried to stay awake because she didn't want to
miss a single minute of this astonishing pleasure. Now
she knew what all the fuss was about, and it thrilled
her beyond imagining that someone as spectacularly
handsome and absolutely marvelous as Clint had been
her first.

And only.

A girl could dream, couldn't she? The fact was,
she loved the man who lay beneath her, taking up
most of the space on a bed the way a big man will.
A big, wonderful man.

She eased back onto her elbows and studied him
in the semidarkness of the wee hours. She loved the
way he slept with just a hint of a smile still on his
face. She loved the way his dark eyelashes curved
over his high cheekbones. She loved his strong jaw
and the sexy cleft in his chin. She loved his black,
black hair, so wiry in texture that after all their love

acrobatics it stood up in tufts like the crown of some virile exotic male bird.

Leaning over she kissed him softly on the lips. He didn't stir. With a tender touch she traced his cheekbones and whispered, ''Thank you'' and ''You're wonderful'' and ''I love you.''

Knowing she was safe because he slept through every one of her declarations.

In spite of her efforts to stay awake and savor every moment she dozed. When the first pale fingers of dawn pinked the windowsill, she startled awake.

Thank goodness she was a farm girl. Thank goodness she got up at first light.

She eased out of his embrace and off the bed. She had a good two hours before the rest of the girls in the dorm would be awake. An additional hour to shower and dress.

She wanted to look good when she withdrew from the pageant. Call it pride. Call it a strong desire not to let Ellie and her dad down. Call it vanity. But just let her get it over with and get on with her life.

Oh, she was excited about her future. Moving away from Hot Coffee. Enrolling in school. Starting a whole 'nother life.

She couldn't wait to tell Sandi.

Clint was still sleeping flat on his back with one arm thrown over his head and the other exactly where she'd placed it. She couldn't leave him like that. She couldn't just walk out without some word.

C.J. found paper and pen in the drawer of the bedside table, then sat in the room's only chair and tried to decide what to say.

''Dear Clint,''

So far, so good. "I'll never forget this night." That was the understatement of the year. "Nor you." Another understatement.

This much she knew: she would love Clint Garrett forever, no matter where she was, no matter what happened.

Putting pen to paper, she wrote, "I am leaving now…"

"C.J.?" Clint sat up, rubbing sleep from his eyes. "What time is it?"

"Early."

He patted the sheets. "Come back to bed. I want to say good morning."

Lord, how she was tempted. But she knew if she climbed back into his bed she wouldn't leave for the next few hours. Not the way he was looking at her. Not the way she was feeling.

"Consider it said."

He glanced at the paper in her hand, then back at her face. "What are you doing?"

"Writing you a note."

"A note?"

"Yes, there are a few things I wanted to say to you before I leave."

"Wait, I'll get my pants and go with you." He jumped out of bed deliciously naked and C.J. almost had a change of heart. "We'll have breakfast, then we'll go and see about getting blood tests."

"Blood tests? It's a little late for that, isn't it?"

"What the devil are you talking about?"

"Last night."

"Last night!" He had one shoe on and one shoe off, but that didn't stop him from stomping around the room waving his arms. She'd never seen a man so mad. "You think I'd do what I did if I had any communicable diseases? Is that what you think?"

"You're the one who mentioned blood tests." When she got mad her nose turned red and her back stiffened as if she had a poker strapped around her ribs. "I surely did not."

"No, but you said *yes.*"

"If memory serves, I said it six times."

"Seven."

They'd been circling each other like fighting roosters, and now they were nose to nose, feathers ruffled beyond redemption, shouting.

"You were *counting?* What kind of man are you?"

"I'm the man you're going to marry."

"Marry? I wouldn't marry you if you were the last man on earth."

"That's right, go off into a temper tantrum and throw my good deed back into my face."

"You consider marrying me a *good deed?*"

"Hadn't you rather be disqualified for something as dignified as marriage than for something scandalous like carousing around drunk after curfew?"

"I was *not* carousing."

"No, but you were drunk."

"I knew exactly what I was doing."

"You were yelling *hell* at the top of your lungs till I stopped you."

"Who's yelling now?"

"You are," he said. "I'm being forceful."

If she hadn't been so mad she'd have laughed. But anger and hurt have a way of burying mirth so deep you wonder if it'll ever surface again.

She sank onto the sex-rumpled sheets, then realized where she was sitting and popped up as if she'd sat in a hive of furious bees. She glanced around the room almost panicked, and Clint brought the chair over and eased her into it with such tenderness she lost all desire to shout.

"So that's what last night was all about," she said. "The pageant."

"Yes. No. Hell, no." He ran a hand through his hair, further spiking it so he looked like a befuddled Statue of Liberty. "I didn't mean that the way it sounded, C.J."

"What did you mean?"

"Here's the thing: you're in trouble and I like you a lot and... What would be so bad about the two of us together?"

"That's it?"

"How creative do you expect me to be at six o'clock in the morning?"

She jumped up and grabbed her bag. She couldn't get out of there fast enough.

"C.J., wait."

She whirled back, both guns blazing. "Wait for what? More insults?"

"I didn't insult you. I'm trying to help you."

"Save it for some other poor unfortunate girl." She stormed across the room and jerked open the door, but he reached around and slammed it shut.

"You can't leave like this."

"Just watch me." She knew she was no match for him, but she tugged at the door on general principles.

"Calm down, C.J. Sit back down and let's talk this out."

"What would you like to talk out? My unfortunate pageant dilemma? Your offer of a mercy marriage?"

"What happened last night…"

"I almost forgot that little misfortune."

"Look, I'm not going to let you make me lose my temper again."

"Oh, I don't think you need any help at all with that. You've a natural ability to roar."

"That's not what you thought last night."

His smile was endearing, his tone cajoling. She almost capitulated. Almost…

"If that's your idea of an olive branch, it stinks. Open that door and let me out of here."

He looked so stricken she might have forgiven him if she hadn't understood his motives. Wounded male pride, that's what motivated Clint Garrett.

"I thought last night was a honeymoon," he said.

Memories washed over her and she nearly died on the spot. If she tried to reply she would surely cry.

Lifting her chin she stared at him until he folded. Without another word he opened the door then stepped back.

Morning hit her in the face like a hot brick. It must be ninety degrees outside. It was going to be a miserable day, which more than suited C.J. She wanted something else to be miserable about. She wanted to wail in pain and wallow in self-pity.

Head held high, she sailed into the day. All the way down the corridor she hoped he'd call her back. She longed for him to run after her and say, "C.J., I didn't mean any of that. Let's start all over."

But there was nothing from Room 414 except dead silence. By the time she turned the corner, she'd lost all hope. Love wasn't fixing to rise from the ashes she'd left behind. The hero wasn't about to change the heroine's mind with a kiss.

And you could bet the heroine wasn't about to turn back and say, "Let's make up and at least be friends."

In the distance the clock tolled the hour. Thirty more minutes and the campus would be astir with hopeful girls. Every last one of them harboring a dream of winning, and only one destined to make it come true.

Amazing how dreams can change so quickly. Amazing how one night can alter the course of a life.

C.J. held herself together until she saw the camellia bushes where he'd first said he was taking her with him, then her tears started.

Funny how dozens of important words can be said but in the end you only remember six or seven.

I thought last night was a honeymoon, he'd said.

"I did, too," she whispered. "Oh, I did, too."

Chapter Twenty

If C. J. Maxey thought he was going to buy champagne and roses then get down on his knees and propose, she didn't know Clint Garrett. Wasn't it enough that he was willing to save her the embarrassment of earning a *reputation* that would follow her the rest of her life? Wasn't it enough that he was willing to sacrifice his freedom in order to rescue her?

She ought to be thanking her lucky stars that he wasn't the kind of man to hold a grudge. She ought to be happy he wasn't the kind of man to go back on his word. He'd said he'd marry her, and by George that's what he was going to do.

First he'd let her cool off. Maybe then he could talk some sense into her.

He climbed into the shower and turned the water on so cold it stung; then he dressed and had a leisurely breakfast, ham and eggs and grits plus three buttered biscuits with strawberry jam.

Sex always made him hungry. The better the sex, the hungrier he got. Shoot, he was liable to get fat after the wedding.

He left the motel's restaurant whistling and was still turning heads with his happy tune when he entered the campus. It would be a while before the pageant activities cranked up again, which gave him time to find C.J. and get things straight.

He was almost to her dorm when a little flower shop on the corner across the street caught his eye. Well, why not?

"I want a dozen of your very best pink roses." What woman could resist roses? C.J. would melt. "Long-stemmed," he said, all of a sudden feeling romantic.

He could do that, too, play the romantic hero. Women liked that sort of thing, didn't they? A little pretense wouldn't hurt him. Besides, C.J. made it easy for a man to feel heroic. Shoot, she even made it fun.

Come to think about it, this whole marriage idea might turn out to be fun.

He walked into her dormitory with his huge floral offering and a big satisfied tomcat's grin on his face.

"C. J. Maxey," he told the dorm mother.

"C.J.?"

"You know… That classy-looking woman with the regal bearing and the extraordinary eyes. Blue. Cheekbones like knife blades, dark feathery hair."

"You just missed her."

It was only a small hitch in his plan. "No problem. I'll catch her at the auditorium."

"She's not there."

"Is she sick?"

"No, she's gone home."

"Home? Back to Hot Coffee?"

"Yes. Her chaperone picked her up about thirty minutes ago."

For an insane moment Clint thought about racing out and hopping on his motorcycle, then striking out after them. He could catch them somewhere up the Trace.

And get a speeding ticket.

And make a fool of himself.

What was it to him if C. J. Maxey wanted to be the most stubborn woman on the face of the earth? What was it to him if she wanted to leave her reputation in shambles?

He thought about throwing the roses in the wastebasket, but his mother had taught him frugality.

"Here." He handed the roses to the dorm mother. "These are for you."

"My goodness. Are you sure?"

"Yes. I won't be needing them anymore."

By the time he arrived at the auditorium, rehearsals were already in progress. He dreaded going in. C.J. would be the talk of the pageant.

Maybe he could put some kind of spin on her activities to soften the story a bit.

Not that she deserved his help. She'd spurned it once. It would serve her right if he left her reputation hanging out there for the newsmongers to rip apart.

The first person he saw was C.J.'s red-haired roommate, her eyes and cheeks bright with excitement.

"I suppose you've heard about C.J.," Gabby told him.

"Everybody must be talking."

"Oh, they are. Nothing like this has ever happened."

"I don't know. There was that girl who got kicked out for doing a nude centerfold."

Why he felt compelled to defend her was beyond him. What he ought to do was let her stew in her own juices.

"Yes," Gabby said. "But this is different."

"I don't see how people can criticize C.J. for doing something that's perfectly natural."

"Oh, nobody's criticizing her. They're just astonished, that's all. It took a lot of courage to do what she did."

Courage to break a few silly rules? Clint must be missing something.

Long ago he'd discovered the best way to find out the truth was to shut up and *listen.* If he hadn't been so busy breaking his own rules, he'd already know what had happened with C. J. Maxey.

"Yes, it did," he said, nodding and trying to look wise and understanding. "C.J. has guts."

"I mean…here she was, the front-runner, and she just ups and withdraws from the pageant."

"Amazing," he said. "You must have mixed feelings."

"I do. See, that puts me ahead now, and, I don't know, I think C.J. did it partly because of me, but what she told the pageant officials was that she doesn't believe her background qualifies her to represent the dairy industry and that our state deserves someone who understands the area of dairy science firsthand.''

"You heard all this from…?''

"I've heard it from just about everybody in this room, that's all the girls can talk about, but no, she wrote a note.''

"She gave the officials a note?''

"Actually, she wrote out what she was going to say to them, then practiced on me.''

"You wouldn't happen to have that note, would you?''

C.J. had never expected to make the headlines, but there she was on the front page. "Front-runner Gracefully Bows Out,'' the headline read.

The writer's byline leaped off the page. *Clint.* Silly, romantic fool that she was, she kissed her fingertips then traced his name.

He'd written beautiful things about her in the article, which didn't surprise her at all now that she'd put some distance between them, now that she'd had time to simmer down and reflect.

The words blurred as she reread the piece. Her father walked through the den and said, "Anything interesting?''

Holding the paper in front of her face, she wiped her eyes. "Not much,'' she said.

"I'm headed to Ellie's.''

"Have a good time.''

"You can count on it.''

She didn't even feel jealous. How could she? She'd been numb ever since she left Jackson yesterday.

"Dad? Before you go, there's something I'd like to talk to you about."

Sam settled into his favorite easy chair. "Fire away."

"Maybe this is callous youth talking and maybe you're going to say it's none of my business, but you and Ellie aren't getting any younger."

Sam laughed. "It's your business because we're a family, and you're right. Ellie and I aren't young anymore, but that doesn't stop us from having a heck of a wonderful time together."

"That's just what I mean. It doesn't make sense for the two of you to live in separate houses. One of you should move in with the other. It'd save a lot of wear and tear on both of you. All this racing back and forth."

"What brought all this discussion on?"

"Well, I'll be gone soon…and maybe I'm finally growing up."

She didn't fool her father for a minute. Sam polished his glasses, a sure sign he was concentrating on what he considered a problem.

"Crystal Jean, you haven't been yourself since you came back from Jackson. Is there anything you'd like to talk to me about?"

"No, Dad. I have a lot on my mind, that's all."

"Okay. If you change your mind, you know where to find me."

"Give Ellie a kiss for me."

"You bet I will," he said, then he was out the door and for the first time since her return she had the house all to herself. A dangerous thing for a woman in her condition.

C.J. felt raw, all nerve endings and very little brain. Every time she thought of being in Clint's arms, which was practically every waking moment, she got giddy and nostalgic and even hopeful. Where there was that much passion, surely there was love.

But if he'd felt love, wouldn't he have said so? Of course he would, which led her to one conclusion: the night that would live forever in her memory was nothing more than another rescue mission to him.

Chapter Twenty-One

Two weeks after Gabrielle Jones won the dairy princess crown, all hell broke loose in Mississippi's dairy industry. And all because of Clint Garrett.

While covering the dairy princesses he'd uncovered one of the biggest scandals to hit the state. The pageant's director, Leroy Levant, was up to his neck in dairy kickbacks on both the state and national level. Several prominent politicians were involved in the scheme, including Senator Marcus Tobias whose daughter was the anonymous *source*. Using information she provided, Clint bulldogged the story until he had enough evidence to break it wide open.

The story broke in the little-known weekly in Hot Coffee then was picked up by the likes of the *Washington Post*. Wayne, bursting with pride and new-found notoriety, traveled down the Natchez Trace

Parkway to Jackson to talk with his former ace reporter.

They sat in lawn chairs on the postage stamp-sized
deck of Clint's recently rented apartment sipping
bloody Mary's although it was only two in the afternoon.

"You're now the hottest reporter in the state,"
Wayne said, and Clint replied in his typical, laid-back
fashion.

"I guess so."

"Hell, I *know* so."

The silence that fell over them was comfortable and
easy, the kind that happens only when two good
friends get together. As always when he had nothing
else to do but think, Clint cogitated on C. J. Maxey.

He wondered where she was and what she was doing and whether she was thinking of him. And *what*
she was thinking of him. Whatever it was, it was
probably venomous.

She'd been madder than a 'coon cornered by hound
dogs when she left.

There was just no pleasing some women.

Wayne shifted his feet onto the deck's railing,
tipped back his head and studied the sun. "It's getting
late."

He didn't have to say, "I'll soon be going." Clint
knew, so all he did was say, "Yep."

Though Wayne had no schedules to keep and no
one waiting for him at home, he was a man in love
with routine. He watched the ten o'clock news, then
poured himself a bourbon and Coke and settled into
his nest, which consisted of four pillows stacked on

the right side of his bed within easy reach of the latest novel he was reading.

He would read till eleven-thirty and then put out the lights, no matter if he was right in the middle of the most interesting scene in the book, even if he was in the middle of murder.

Everybody who knew Wayne Vaughn knew his routine. He told it every year at the office Christmas party, and that was the extent of his socializing.

Driving three hundred miles out of his way for a visit was rare for the editor of the *Hot Coffee Tribune*. The visit was a tribute to their friendship as well as to Clint's heretofore hidden talent.

"I guess you'll be leaving soon, yourself," Wayne said.

"Maybe."

"That's some mighty attractive offers you got."

Clint didn't say anything. Every time he tried to envision himself working at a big paper in Chicago or Atlanta or Washington, he felt such a sense of emptiness he wondered if he might be coming down with a serious disease.

Heart problems.

It could happen. Men younger than he had died from failed hearts.

"Decided which one you'll take yet?"

"I'm still mulling it over."

"Don't wait too long. Lightning might not strike twice." Wayne stood up and shook his hand. "You're always welcome at the *Tribune*, but nothing would make me happier than to see the taillights of your Harley disappearing in the direction of Atlanta.

There're some mighty good newsmen over there. A man could go places and learn a lot.''

So far the only place Clint could think about going was a certain little yellow house in Hot Coffee, Mississippi, which was proof of only one thing: C. J. Maxey was some kind of witch. Obviously she'd cast a spell over him.

He knew his obsession with her would peter out in a few days. After all, he'd never kept a woman in his mind longer than the time it took her to get out the door and down the road a piece.

What he needed was to find a good fishing hole and sit on the bank for a while until his natural wandering instincts took over again. Then he'd be free to strike out wherever the notion took him.

Maybe he'd go to Atlanta, give big-city life and heavy-duty reporting a whirl. Nothing was holding him in Mississippi.

Nothing except a sassy woman he couldn't seem to forget.

The only person who knew what had happened the night before C.J. withdrew from the dairy princess pageant was Sandi, and she didn't know the particulars. All she knew was that C.J. needed her now as never before, and for the rest of the summer she was in the Maxey house more than in her own.

Sandi stopped accepting work that would take her out of town. Instead she stayed in Hot Coffee photographing weddings and painting portraits and making sure that C.J. was too busy to mourn her lost love.

But her efforts were in vain. As long as Sam was in the house C.J. pretended perkiness, but as soon as he was out the door she fell into a deep sorrow that nothing could cure.

"Nobody ever died of a broken heart," she told C.J.

They were standing in the middle of C.J.'s bedroom sorting through clothes deciding what C.J. would take to school and what she would leave behind.

"It doesn't feel that way."

"How well I know. Of course, in hindsight I'll have to say that I never *loved* any of the men I was going to marry." Sandi held up a pair of faded jeans that happened to be C.J.'s favorites, then tossed them into the discard pile. "I *thought* I did, though, and that's what counts."

"My situation is not like yours, Sandi. I really do love Clint Garrett." C.J. rescued her jeans and tossed them into a suitcase.

"How can you be sure? Maybe you only think you do because he was your first. Women are often sentimental about their first."

"I just *know,* that's all."

"Yes, but how do you know?"

C.J. wished for her mother's common sense, Ellie's wisdom and even Dolly's self-assurance, but all she had to guide her was a night of paradise and a heart on fire.

"If it's true love, it's magic. That's how I know."

And having known she could never settle for less.

C.J. glanced around the room that had been her haven for twenty-five years. Leaving was bittersweet.

"Don't worry, C.J. Your dad's in good hands."

"I know."

"You'll be less than a hundred miles from home."

"It already seems like more."

"I'll come down when I can to visit, and you'll be home often."

"It's not that."

"What, then?"

"I feel as if I'm saying goodbye to a whole way of life."

"In a way, you are." Sandi took her hands. "I know I can never take the place of Phoebe or Ellie, and I know I'm not very wise, but I have learned a few things from my travels and my *many* failed relationships. When you walk away from one thing, you're walking toward another."

Chapter Twenty-Two

The main problem with choosing a new city and a different newspaper and getting on with his life was that Clint had a few loose ends to tie up in his old one. Namely C. J. Maxey.

She hadn't vanished from his mind. If anything, she'd gotten stronger.

Everything would have been okay if she'd gone along with his plan, but *no,* she had to go off on a tangent and refuse to see reason. What she'd done was destroy his peace of mind.

Until he saw her and set things right, there was no way he could have a future. He was a man in limbo.

Even fishing couldn't rescue him. Even drinking and shooting pool and trying to pick up other women didn't work because while he hadn't been looking the other women had all turned into silly, simpering sheep wearing too much eye makeup and not enough clothes.

Furthermore, he couldn't drink enough to drown C.J., and he lost so many billiard games he was laughed out of the pool hall.

And so one fine September morning he packed a duffel bag and struck out on his motorcycle for Hot Coffee. He didn't have a plan but he did have a goal: to marry C. J. Maxey.

He stopped in Shady Grove for lunch, then on impulse bought a dozen roses—red this time because pink didn't seem to work very well—and a bottle of cheap champagne.

Cheap because he hadn't earned a paycheck in six weeks, and although he was borderline famous that still didn't make him rich. Or even successful.

By the time he got to Hot Coffee he was sweating profusely, partially because it was one of those hotter-than-the-hinges-of-hell September days that acted more like July, but mostly because he was nervous.

Any man in his shoes would be. Face it, he was fixing to propose to a woman who had already turned him down once. Plus, he didn't even know what he was going to say.

He guessed he'd let the roses and champagne do the talking for him. Women liked that kind of thing. Shoot, if C.J. had seen his pink roses she might have changed her mind.

Maybe he'd made a mistake getting red instead of pink. Maybe he ought to drive back over to Shady Grove and get some pink ones just in case.

He was still vacillating between going back and

going on when the yellow house leaped out at him. Too late to turn back now.

Before he killed the engine he could tell no one was home. The house had a deserted look. Too, his instincts told him that C.J. was nowhere near.

Wasn't that just his luck? The champagne was getting lukewarm, the roses were wilting and he wasn't far from it himself.

Maybe something he ate in Shady Grove didn't agree with him. Maybe the idea of marriage didn't agree with him.

If he had a lick of sense he'd give the roses to the next woman he met, drink the champagne and head to someplace as far away from Hot Coffee as he could get.

Maybe Alaska. Where it was cool. Where there were no dairy princesses, accidental or otherwise.

"Clint?" Sandi appeared out of nowhere. "I saw the motorcycle and guessed it might be you."

"Where'd you come from?"

"Through the hedge." She laughed. "C.J. and I made that path between our houses when we were children." She looked at the roses and her face lit up. "You're looking for C.J!"

"Yes. Do you know where she is?"

"She's in Starkville. In school."

Good news for her, bad for him. Or maybe not. Maybe Sandi was the voice of Fate saying, Keep on going.

"She got a marvelous scholarship," Sandi added. "That plus a student loan and a part-time job in the campus bookstore will see her through."

''So she's an independent woman now? Good for her.''

''She has her own apartment. I can give you her address.''

He meant to say, ''Don't bother,'' but what he actually said was, ''Where does she live?''

Fifteen minutes later he was twenty miles down the road heading back the way he'd come, calling himself fifty different kinds of fool.

Thirty minutes down the road he was still telling himself he could take any turn he wanted to and head in the other direction.

Five minutes later he stopped at a service station to get some fresh water for those aggravating little plastic doodads the rose stems were in, and ten minutes after that he stopped at another one to ice down the champagne. He bought a Mars bar and sat on a rickety picnic bench for thirty minutes while the champagne cooled off. Then he hopped on his Harley and tore out for Starkville.

There was no turning back now.

When C.J. first heard the roar of a motorcycle she told herself not to be silly, that it couldn't possibly be Clint Garrett. She went back to folding her laundry, then as the roar came closer instinct propelled her across the room where she eased back the curtain and tried to see out. Unfortunately an overgrown tea olive bush was in the way.

Any sane woman would have gone back to her laundry, but where Clint was concerned, C.J. was not sane. She raced into the bathroom to wash her face and comb her hair. As if it mattered.

Even if Clint did show up on her doorstep, he'd surely be up to no good.

The motorcycle ground to a stop and so did C.J.'s heart. When her doorbell rang she couldn't move. What if it was Clint? What would she say?

What if it wasn't? Would she die of disappointment?

The bell rang again. It *was* Clint. She sensed his presence even before she opened the door.

She nearly cried when she saw him. Never had a man looked so wonderful. And when he smiled at her, she floated two feet off the floor on secret wings unfurling beneath her T-shirt.

"Hello, Clint."

"Hello, C.J."

They stared at each other the way intimate almost-strangers will, long and deep. Their thoughts hovered above them, screaming, drowning out any possibility of speech.

Paralysis slowly left C.J. and she swung open the door. Clint followed her inside, a tall, well-built man who made the apartment seem tiny. She took a straight-backed chair near the window, and he sat on the sofa with his knees bumping the coffee table.

"I brought these for you."

The roses he held out for her drooped and gasped on stems he'd squeezed within an inch of their life.

"They are wonderful. Thank you."

Her eyes got tangled up with his again and she had to look away. Burying her face in the blossoms she took a deep, steadying breath while she tried to figure out the meaning of flowers. It wasn't her birthday, it wasn't Valentine's or Christmas or Easter.

Men didn't bring flowers unless they were serious, did they? Of course, Clint was not any man. Flowers could mean anything to him or nothing at all. They could mean...

"Are you going to smell the roses all day or are you going to look at me?"

She looked, and discovered that looking was dangerous. Every erotic dream she'd had of him for the last six weeks sprang to life, and she wanted to race across the room and throw herself into his arms. She wanted to moan and scream and carry on like a woman dying of love. Which she was.

"I'm looking."

"You don't have to bite my head off."

"I'm not snarling. That's just my natural personality shining through."

"Try shining a little less."

"Try judging a little less."

Great. He'd been here less than five minutes and already they were at each other's throats. When there was so much to be said between them, why couldn't C.J. curb her sharp tongue for just three minutes and let him talk? Why couldn't she be meek and mild and gentle and tell him exactly how she felt?

"Look, I'm sorry, C.J. We got off on the wrong foot."

"Again."

"Yeah, again."

The endearing way he smiled could break a woman's heart. And did. C.J. heard pieces of hers falling.

"Why don't I put these in water, then when I come

back we'll pretend you've just walked in the door and we'll start all over.''

"Deal."

In the kitchen for no reason at all she started to cry. Grabbing a dish towel she wiped her tears and swore she'd do better.

She didn't have a proper vase to put the roses in, so she washed a peanut butter jar she'd emptied at lunch. She tried to peel the label off but most of it got stuck and wouldn't budge. Since she didn't want to spend the rest of the afternoon in the kitchen thinking dirty words to an inanimate object, she went back into the den carrying Clint's wilting floral offering as if it were the crown jewels of England.

"They look great," she said.

"So do you."

"Thanks."

She headed back to her chair but he patted the sofa and said, "Please. Sit beside me."

"Okay. But I'm warning you. I'm not sure I can control myself."

She'd meant her statement to be light, her laughter to be bright and happy and carefree. But then he looked into her soul and she looked into his and they were in each other's arms kissing as if they were warriors returned from the battlefront, kissing as if they could never get enough of each other, kissing as if there was *forever* and it belonged exclusively to them.

Logic vanished until they pulled apart for air, then C.J. knew a million things she wanted to tell him: I've missed you, I need you, I want you, I'm sorry. But most of all I love you.

And, oh, he had to love her back. His kisses told her so.

She opened her mouth to speak, but he pressed his fingertip to her lips.

"C.J., I think we should get married."

"You *think* we should get married."

"Yes. That's what I said."

"Yes, that's exactly what you said."

She was so mad she couldn't sit still. And she certainly didn't want to sit by him with his leg touching hers making her crazy and his body heat zapping her like electrical currents and his big, *big*... Oh, she was furious. Jumping up, she stomped to the other side of the room and sat in her chair ramrod straight.

"What did I say?"

He was a good actor. She'd grant him that. He looked as befuddled as a baby bird taking its maiden flight. But she wasn't about to waste sympathy on him. The Clint Garretts of the world always landed on their feet.

"You know exactly what you said."

Her conscience didn't even hurt when she snarled this time, not one little twinge. Here she was, a foolish, fanciful woman who had built her hopes up because of a few bedraggled roses. Here she'd been thinking he'd had a chance to search his heart and soul and come up with the logical conclusion that he loved her.

"What did I do wrong this time?" When he got up he bumped his knee on the corner of the coffee table. "Dammit. Whoever built this froufrou furniture ought to be shot."

"My great-grandfather Maxey built it. That table's an antique, handed down by generations of Maxeys."

He looked as if he wanted to strangle her venerable ancestor with his bare hands. Instead he stalked to the window and stood there with his back to her.

When he whirled back around his eyes were blazing. "You want me to get down on my knees? Is that it?"

Before she could answer he was kneeling in front of her, stealing every bit of the air in the room. With her knees crushed against his chest and her hands buried in his, she thought she would faint.

"Look, I know I'm bullheaded and contrary and not very successful, but dammit, C.J., I took your innocence! There's no reason in the world for you to tell me *no.*"

"Is that what this proposal is all about? My stupid virginity?"

"It wasn't stupid. It was kind of sweet."

"Don't try to con me." She jerked her hands out of his and shoved him backward. "Get up off your feet and march right out of my house."

"Hell, C.J., I just asked you to marry me."

"No, you didn't. You asked me to salve your conscience. You broke your code and slept with a virgin and now you're feeling guilty."

He didn't deny it. Darned his wretched hide, if only he would deny it.

"You're turning me down twice?"

"You've got it, hotshot."

"What did I do wrong?"

"Haven't you ever heard of romance?"

"I bought a dozen red roses. Long-stemmed."

"Flowers usually come with sentiments."

"I told you my sentiments. We're both starting a new life and we could have a good time together. Besides, there's not as many good women out there as there used to be and neither one of us is getting any younger."

"Are you calling me an old maid?"

"I didn't say that."

"You are the most…" She threw up her hands. "I can't even talk to you. I *don't want* to talk to you. Leave."

He didn't budge. As a matter of fact, he looked as if he might be going to do something drastic. Such as kiss her.

If he kissed her again, all was lost. Passion would drown out the finer sentiments, and she'd enter into a union with a stubborn but devilishly charming man who didn't know the first thing about love and would probably never learn. She'd be doomed.

C.J. jerked up the peanut butter jar and shoved it at him.

"And take your flowers with you."

He did.

She rushed to the window so she could watch until he was out of sight, but the tea olive bush saved her. Instead of watching Clint Garrett disappear from her life, C.J. went to her ironing board, attacked her laundry and burned a hole in her favorite pink blouse.

Clint pulled over to the side of the road and tossed the roses into the first cow pasture he saw.

"Good riddance," he said.

He was through with roses, through with romance,

through with C. J. Maxey. A man who had been turned down twice by the same woman knew when to fold his cards and quit the game. Clint Garrett was quitting. Yessirree, he'd be happy if he never laid eyes on another woman. They were nothing but trouble.

It began to get dark and his stomach began to rumble, so he pulled over at a truck stop and ordered a logger's meal—ham and peas and fried okra with plenty of cornbread and all the coffee he could drink.

He needed caffeine. He needed to stay awake. Where he was going, he didn't know. All he knew was that he meant to travel far and travel fast.

He might even go back to Reform, Alabama. See if he liked it. If he did, he'd move all his stuff from Jackson and stay in Alabama a spell. Forget about a new job. Forget about making something of himself.

And definitely forget about marriage.

The waitress—Irma Doris her name tag read—set his food on the table, and while she was pouring tea she said, "I like your shirt, hon."

"Thank you."

"It makes them big ole blue peepers of yours just stand out like headlights."

He'd worn the shirt especially for C.J., not that it had done a bit of good. "I'm glad somebody likes it," he said, and then Irma Doris pursed her mouth in sympathy and said, "Had a bad day, hon?"

"The best thing about this day is, it's over."

Hot food and a sympathetic listener put him in a better mood, but as soon as he hit the open road again he fell back into a blue funk.

"It had to be the shirt," he said. C.J. didn't like

plaid. That was it. If he'd worn his blue shirt or even a striped one, she might have said yes.

Shoot, plaid wasn't natural. Nature was full of stripes, and even polka dots, but he couldn't think of a single animal that was plaid. If God had meant for a man to wear plaid, he'd have given him checkered skin.

Clint pulled off the road onto a dirt lane leading nowhere he could see, then stripped off the unlucky plaid shirt and pulled on a T-shirt. He'd show C. J. Maxey.

Why, women would be crawling all over him. Not that he planned to notice. From now on he was wearing blinders.

He roared down the dirt road a while to see what he could discover, and when he'd gone twenty miles without seeing a single house, he turned around and went back to the highway.

Pretty soon he'd be to the state line. He could cross over or veer north or even go south again if he wanted. Avoiding Starkville altogether. He was never setting foot in that town again.

A moon as big as a galleon rose over Alabama and rode the night sky, and Venus was so big and bright she looked like you could take a flying leap and be sitting right on top of her.

Clint decided to pull off the road into the welcome station that straddled the Mississippi/Alabama line. He'd pop the cork on the not-so-celebratory champagne and drink every bit of it himself. Then he'd bed down beside his motorcycle and sleep under the stars.

It was only after he'd parked under a spreading oak

tree that he discovered he'd left the champagne in Starkville. With C.J.

That one little thought opened the floodgates and she roared through his blood like a river. With the lover's moon overhead and Venus winking a wicked, knowing eye, Clint came unhinged by love.

Until that very moment he'd called love *nonsense,* the dreams of deluded men and foolish women, the stuff of nightmares and divorces. He'd denied its very existence.

But he was wrong. Every bone in his body ached with it. Every breath he drew sang with it. Every beat of his heart affirmed it.

When he wasn't looking he'd fallen in love. When he'd let down his guard, C. J. Maxey had stolen his heart.

Now he understood her anger. No wonder she'd turned him down. He was lucky she hadn't whopped him upside the head with the champagne bottle.

It wasn't the plaid shirt that had done him in; it was his own foolish pride, his arrogance, his hubris. When he thought about his ridiculous posturing, his yammering about a marriage built on a mild regard and the possibility of a few laughs, he started laughing and couldn't stop.

He laughed so hard a couple who'd obviously been necking in the back seat of their Honda Civic rose up in disgust and drove away. On the heels of his laughter came a need that drove him to his knees.

He had to have roses, he had to have chilled champagne, he had to have relief.

Clint climbed back on his Harley and started south once more, straining his eyes through the darkness for any sign of a florist's shop, even an all-night grocery story that might sell fresh flowers.

He was out of luck. Small towns in Mississippi shut down after dark, especially on a Monday night when the owners could be home watching Monday night football.

By the time he reached the outskirts of Starkville it was after midnight and he still didn't have roses. On his left a cow pasture was coming up, one he recognized as the dumping ground for his roses.

Clint coasted to a stop. Well, why not? If the cows hadn't had a high-priced feast the flowers might still be there. Probably a little worse for wear, but the stems were in those dinky plastic holders, so how bad could they be?

They might still be fresh-looking. Especially in the dark.

Clint found his flashlight, climbed over the barbed wire fence and stepped right into a bed of fire ants. Hollering and carrying on, he stripped off his pants, dropped to the ground and rolled right into a haystack.

The bull on the other side had been minding his own business till a madman plowed into his hay. He took umbrage and gave chase. Clint leaped over the fence and tore his arm and still didn't have his roses.

They faced off, a determined man in his blue plaid boxer shorts and a mad bull wearing a perfectly good pair of Levis on his horns.

"If you think I'm leaving without my roses, you don't know me."

While the bull pawed the pasture, Clint pawed

through his gear looking for another pair of pants. Alas! All he found was a pair of blue striped pajama bottoms. He put them on. For he was going courting and nothing was going to stop him!

Chapter Twenty-Three

C.J. found the lukewarm champagne about nine o'clock. Though she knew Clint had left it behind she figured her guardian angel had a hand in the oversight because how else was she going to get through the rest of the evening without dying of love?

She didn't even own a corkscrew, so she found a paring knife and set to work. After much to-do she uncorked the bottle and got only a little bit of cork down in the champagne. Then she poured herself a glass and made a toast.

"To every woman over twenty-five and looking. Don't look Clint Garrett's way. He doesn't believe in love."

She took a big swig and choked. "Slow down, old girl, you've got all evening."

Kicking off her shoes, she piled all the pillows on

one end of the sofa and stretched out. She might as well get prone right away. With her head for alcohol she'd be that way after half a glass, anyhow.

She took another drink, a small sip this time, then started giggling and couldn't stop.

Figuring that laughter was much better for her soul than tears, she refilled her glass while she still could, then set about drinking and giggling.

The next thing she knew she was jarred out of sleep by a commotion outside. She bolted off the bed and crashed into the coffee table.

She wasn't in bed at all but on her sofa in a wrinkled wad with her head sweating from being buried in pillows and her feet cold from having no cover.

Now that she was awake the ruckus outside took on definition. Somebody was dying out there with a great deal of suffering, and they'd set out to make her suffer, too. Every moan and wail went straight to C.J.'s throbbing head.

She put a finger to her lips. "Shh," she said as she stumbled toward the door. Leaving the chain on she opened it just a crack. "Pipe down out there."

"C.J.?"

There was a shadow on her porch that looked like a man, but in her condition she couldn't be sure. It could have been an elephant. Pink.

"Clint?"

"Open up and let me in. I've been out here banging and hollering for thirty minutes."

"What gall!" C.J. barreled out, fists and feet flying.

"Quit that, C.J., ouch! Now stop that!"

The small stoop wasn't designed to accommodate

a wrestling match. They lurched off the porch, air-borne. The tussling lovers landed in a tangled heap in the tea olive bush.

Clint cushioned her fall but C.J. was in no mood to thank him. Spinsters offered mercy marriages tend to be surly if not downright pugilistic.

She doubled up her fist and took aim at his eye, but he caught her wrist.

"Now, be still. I've got something to tell you."

"Ha!"

He'd already said enough to consign him to purgatory for the next two hundred years. Her knee was just right so she took aim, planning to ram it where it hurt the most.

Clint rolled to the side, then rolled back and pinned her underneath him. She started squirming, then suddenly stopped. Awed.

"Where are your pants?" she asked.

"Somewhere in Starkville there's a very well-dressed bull." Sensing the fight had gone out of her, he said, "Are you ready to listen to me now?"

"What else can I do? I'm on the bottom and you're on top."

"Don't remind me." He spoke through gritted teeth.

Good. It was no fun to be the only one in a precarious situation. Let him twist in the winds of desire. She wanted him, but he didn't love her and she wasn't about to settle for less.

"Well? What's so all-fired important that you had to interrupt my sleep and the whole neighborhood at this god-awful hour?"

"You sleep in your clothes?"

"Sometimes."

He leaned down and sniffed. "You've been drinking."

"I have not."

"Yes, you have."

"Maybe. Just a teensy weensy bit."

He roared with laughter, then did the craziest thing. He plastered himself all over her and gave her a kiss that made every sane thought she had fly right out of her head.

"I love you, C.J."

Naturally he didn't say that. Her mind was playing tricks. It was the champagne talking. And her wishful thinking.

"Did you hear me? I said, I love you."

"You're confessing to a romantic sentiment?"

"Yes."

"You just said you love me."

"Yes, I did." He kissed her again in a way that proved it. Nearly.

When she came up for air she said, "Better try that again. I'm not sure you mean it."

His hearty boom of laughter startled two cats on the fence that surrounded the apartment and they set up a yowling that had neighbors slamming windows and yelling, "Quiet out there."

"I can't kiss you again," he said.

"Why not?"

"Once I start I don't plan to stop."

"Don't stop."

She tried to pull him back down but he wouldn't budge.

"C.J., if we don't get out of these bushes I'm going to ruin your reputation."

"Ruin it."

Instead he picked her up and struggled out of the tea olive. The minute they got inside they fell upon each other like starving travelers who'd stumbled into a field of ripe corn.

Swaying and kissing and moaning, she reached for his shirt and he reached for her shorts. Clothes trailed behind them as they moved in lock-step in the direction of the bedroom.

They made it as far as the sofa. When he was finally buried deep inside her, she exhaled with pleasure and relief. At long last she could believe this was really happening to her. Finally she knew the truth: his love was true and real and lasting.

She could give herself completely now, for he would still be there in the morning. And the morning after that and on into eternity. Clint Garrett would still be at her side loving her.

"I love you," she whispered. "I love you."

"I love you, too," he said, and then he took her on a journey to the moon that left them both sated and sweating.

"Does this place have a bedroom?" he asked.

"Yes."

"To be continued."

"I don't want to move."

"You don't have to." He picked her up and said, "Which way?"

"Second star to the right," she said.

"Peter Pan."

"You know him?"

"I *am* him." Holding her hard against his chest he kissed her. "Or was." He kissed her again. "Until today."

"Don't stop now."

"I don't know if I can kiss and walk at the same time. But I'm sure going to try."

And he did. Kissing and laughing and stumbling they took their time getting to the bedroom. Clint lowered her to the mattress then bent over and brushed her sweat-damp hair from her face.

"You are so beautiful. I want to see you."

He switched on the light...and she screamed.

"Good heavens. What happened to you?"

Red welts the size of copper pennies dotted his legs, a long scratch angled down his arm and bits of hay clung to his hair.

He started laughing. "Good lord, I forgot."

"You forgot?"

"Wait right there. I'll be right back." He tore off and left her lolling on the bed, as sleek and satisfied as a Persian cat who has just stolen the tuna.

She didn't want to move from that spot. And she didn't plan to for a very long time.

"I'm back."

Clint stood in the doorway holding the worst-looking roses she'd ever seen. The petals were crushed and bruised, the stems bent and broken, the leaves stripped bare. The bouquet looked as if had left the peanut butter jar then gone to war with six mad dogs and seven angry cats.

"These are for you," he said.

"Those are the most beautiful roses in the world,"

she said, and meant it. What had earlier been a meaningless gesture was now a gift of the heart.

Without moving from the doorway he said, "Here's what happened to me. I was racing down the road trying to get as far away from you as I could when all of a sudden the moon came out of Alabama and tapped me on the shoulder and Venus winked, and I was unhinged by love. Struck speechless. Brought to my knees."

C.J. held her breath and listened with all her heart. Magic came only once in a lifetime, and at long last it had come to her.

"Love couldn't have been clearer if a thunderbolt had scrawled it across the sky."

Now he started moving toward the bed. Breathless with expectation and love, C.J. watched while he laid the roses on the bedside table and sank onto the mattress. She didn't move when he smoothed back her hair and caressed her cheek with his knuckles.

"I knew that I couldn't let you go, that I can never let you go, and so I turned my Harley around and headed toward you."

Bending down he planted tender kisses on her forehead, her eyes, her cheeks, her lips.

"I couldn't find a florist, so I retrieved the roses at great peril…" She opened her mouth to comment, but he put his fingers to her lips. "…because I want fresh flowers and champagne when I propose…once and for all."

He kissed her softly once more. "Tears?" he whispered, then gathered them with his fingertips and put them in his mouth.

"I'm so silly," she said. "I always cry when I'm happy."

"Good lord, the price of tissue will skyrocket."

"Why?"

"Because I'm making it my life's mission to keep you happy."

He bent to her lips and passion bloomed so quickly they almost forgot about the proposal. He was already tasting her sweet, perky breasts when he murmured, "Will you marry me?"

"Wait," she said. "I'll get the champagne… what's left of it."

"I can't."

"Well…" He drew a taut nipple deep into his mouth and love exploded through her. "Hmm," she murmured, which could have had a dozen different meanings, but mostly it meant, "You are my soul mate, my heart, my universe and I don't need roses and champagne. All I need is you."

Chapter Twenty-Four

With the lights on Clint explored the terrain of love with a tenderness he wouldn't have thought possible until tonight. He discovered a small mole underneath C.J.'s left breast and a star-shaped café-au-lait birthmark high on her right thigh and a dime-sized scar on her left knee. Little things. Loving things. The kind of secrets that make a man pause in the middle of work and smile for no reason at all.

She gasped when he kissed the mole, laughed when he nuzzled the scar, exploded in the best of ways when he licked the birthmark.

He watched her eyes squeeze shut then go wide and soft with wonder.

"Wow!" she said.

"I intend to find all your hot spots," he told her.

"And I intend to find yours."

"I can't wait."

"Neither can I."

She pulled him down to her breasts and made the sweet, murmuring sounds he loved. And when the anticipation became unbearable, he joined them once more and they became liquid fire. A moving, raging river of heat enveloped them until finally they washed ashore, wet and trembling with the awesome power of love.

They didn't talk, but lay with arms and legs tangled together, her head on his chest while he traced her spine with his fingertips. Tenderly, ever so tenderly.

Because she was special. Because he loved her. Because he was her first.

The knowledge that she was his and his alone filled him up and made him whole, made him a better man than he'd ever been or had ever hoped to be. No man had ever touched her as he had. No man had ever made her eyes go wide and her mouth go soft. No man had ever heard her sweet, humming sounds of pleasure and her small screams of completion.

"You make me feel like a god. I don't deserve a woman like you...but I'm certainly going to try."

Plans for the future whirled through his head. There was so much he wanted to tell her, so much he needed to tell her.

"I know we can't get everything said in one night, but I've been thinking about the offers I got and your schooling. You're going to be really busy the next few years studying, and I am going to be busy starting my own newspaper."

He shifted to exactly the right spot, marveling how perfectly they fit together and how wonderful it felt to know he'd go to sleep with her in his arms and wake up exactly the same way.

"I don't really want to live in a big city. I've always fancied small towns, and I was thinking…wouldn't it be great if we bought a piece of property out in the country big enough for a veterinary practice and a couple of dogs and about five kids?

"I'll be a good father. I can promise you that." She didn't answer. "You *do* want children, don't you?" Silence. "C.J.?"

He leaned back to see her face. She was sound asleep, her mouth curved in a soft, satisfied smile.

He kissed her forehead. "I love you, C.J."

The sun was at twelve o'clock high when C.J. woke up. She stretched, catlike, then rolled over to find the other side of her bed empty.

For a moment panic seized her. He'd had second thoughts. He'd vanished on his Harley and she'd never see or hear from him again.

Then she saw the reddened patches on her breasts where his beard had burned her fair skin and felt the delicious warmth where'd he'd spilled his seed. Every sweet, tender word he'd spoken came back to her, and she knew that Clint Garrett was hers for the keeping.

"Clint?" she called.

"In here."

Barefoot and naked, she raced toward the sound of his dear voice.

"Good morning, sleepyhead," he said, and she burst into tears. "I take it you're happy with my surprise."

Overwhelmed, all she could say was, "Ohh."

The shades were drawn and candles were everywhere, their flames shimmering on the glitter that covered the carpet. Roses filled every corner of the room, red and pink with long stems in green florist's vases tied with enormous white ribbons. Heart-shaped balloons bobbed from the ceiling, their messages appearing and disappearing as they did their delirious helium-induced dance.

I love you.

Marry me.

Let me call you sweetheart.

The messages made her cry even harder. Clint brought her a handful of tissue and wiped her face, and that's when she noticed six boxes sitting on the coffee table.

"In case you get any happier," he said, and she laughed through her tears.

"What did you have in mind?"

"This." Holding her hand, he dropped to one knee, then got distracted and spent several heady minutes savoring the spot she'd marked *reserved for Garrett* from the minute she'd laid eyes on him.

Holding on to his hair to stay aloft, she whispered, "I love you, Clint Garrett. I've always loved you."

"Truly?"

"Yes, truly."

"I haven't made much of my life and I don't even know my daddy's name."

"I know your name and I know your love. That's all that counts."

He kissed her hands. "I want you to be my wife. I want to see your dear face when I go to sleep at night and when I wake up in the morning. I want to love you and pamper you and laugh with you the rest of my days. Will you marry me, C.J.?''

"Yes." She fell to her knees where he wrapped her in an embrace that held them heart to heart. "Oh, yes."

"I bought a brand-new bottle of champagne."

"The champagne can wait."

He lowered her to a carpet of stars, and when he thrust home she said, "Yes, yes, yes."

"Third time's a charm," he said.

It was the last word either of them spoke for a very long time.

Chapter Twenty-Five

The bride wore pink. So did the fifteen bridesmaids who had come from all over the country to celebrate the marriage of one of their own.

Fluffing up her ruffles and adjusting her veil, the bride asked, "Do you think this gown's too much?" and Mrs. Clint Garrett replied, "Absolutely not. Daddy will think you're beautiful."

"Oh, I hope so," Ellie said. "I didn't want to wear white because of Phoebe."

She got a faraway look in her eyes, and her sorority sisters immediately circled the wagons, every one of them wearing fierce looks that said, The Foxes protect their own.

"Ellie, the past is over and done with," Dolly Wilder said. "Live in the present, that's what I say."

She'd flown in from London where she was appearing onstage in Shakespeare's *MacBeth*.

"Hear, hear!" Kitty O'Banyon's crazy hat bobbed as she shouted her approval.

Although all the Foxes wore identical pink bridesmaid gowns, they each wore hats of their own choosing, the hallmark broadbrimmed hat reminiscent of their wild and crazy college days. Some were decorated with sequins, some with flowers and feathers, some even sported the American flag.

Kitty's flaunted a bouquet of miniature plastic bottles.

"Kitty, where did you get that ridiculous hat?" Dolly asked.

"Where do you think?" Lucy O'Banyon Coltrane spoke up. "She got it free with a case of tequila."

Amid all the laughter C.J. slipped away and went down the staircase of the vast O'Banyon mansion to check on her dad. Sam was in the library looking nervous while his son-in-law of three weeks adjusted his tie.

"Darling, come reassure your dad," Clint said. "He's more nervous than I was."

C.J. laughed. "Impossible. You dropped the ring."

"I didn't drop it. I wanted to see your legs."

Sam burst out laughing. "I don't know which makes me happier, C.J. Your wedding or my own."

"Both," she said. "I'm equally happy about both."

"Uh-oh, she's happy. Here come the water works." Clint reached into his pocket and pulled out a handkerchief, then circled an arm around his wife's waist and bent over to dab her face. "There you are, Mrs. Garrett. How's that?"

"Kiss it and make it all better."

"Scat. Shoo." Sam waved them out of the room. "We have forty minutes before the wedding. I need some quiet in here so I can have a nervous breakdown."

Clint whisked her down the hall and shut them up in a walnut-paneled office with heavy draperies over the windows and a deep leather sofa. He closed and locked the door then pulled her into his arms.

"Come here, you. I've always hankered to kiss a bridesmaid."

"Just any old bridesmaid?"

"Only the ones in pink."

"That gives you fifteen to choose from. How in the world are you ever going to narrow it down?"

"For starters I'll look to see if there's a little scar on her knee." He slid his hand under her skirts and caressed the small indention on her knee. "So far so good."

"Hmm." C.J. planted soft kisses all over her husband's face, starting with his incredible eyes and ending with his talented lips. "And then?"

"Next I have to find a pretty maid with a star on her thigh."

Clint carried her to the sofa then knelt and gave his full attention to the tiny birthmark just above the tops of her stockings. Suddenly there were skyrockets in her veins and firecrackers along her nerve endings, and as she arched upward on a cry, her husband captured her lips.

"Thank God for thick walls," he said, and she whispered, "And then?"

"Insatiable minx."

"Are you complaining?"

"Bragging." He reached for her zipper and slid her dress off. "And when I find a tiny mole beneath her breast..." He kissed her small mole. "I'll know I have the right woman."

"Do you?" she whispered.

"Yes," he said, and then he slid home.

* * * * *

We hope you love
THE ACCIDENTAL PRINCESS
so much that you share it with friends and
family. If you do—or if you belong to a
book club—there are questions on the next
page that are intended to help you start a
book group discussion. We hope these
questions inspire you and help you get
even more out of the book.

READERS' RING DISCUSSION GROUP QUESTIONS:

1. What are C.J.'s motivations for agreeing to enter the Dairy Princess contest? To what extent do her love/guilt feelings for her mother influence her decision?

2. A hallmark of this Southern author is a fascination with the past. To what extent does the past shape the lives of C.J., Clint, Sam and Ellie? How is this theme reflected in the life of the secondary character Sandi Wentworth?

3. What are the major themes of the book?

4. Although Phoebe is deceased, she plays a major role in THE ACCIDENTAL PRINCESS. What is it? How does she influence C.J., Ellie and Sam?

5.   What major events shaped Clint's character? At what point does he reach an understanding of himself? Of his true feelings for C.J.? Is his epiphany consistent with his character?

6.   Although Clint neither admits nor acknowledges his love for C.J. till near the end of the book, he shows his love in many ways. What are they? To what extent does the prom reflect his understanding of C.J.'s needs?

7.   C.J.'s virginity plays an important role in the story. What is it? How is her innocence important to Clint? Would a non-virgin heroine have had the same impact on him? Why or why not?

8.   How do C.J.'s external changes reflect the metamorphosis of her character?

9.   At what point in the book does C.J. experience epiphanies regarding love and her own life? Are they consistent with her character?

10.   Why does Clint go to such extremes to take roses to C.J. when he proposes? What is the symbolism of the battered roses he eventually takes to her?

11.   Ellie plays multiple roles. What are they? How is she important to C.J.? To Sam?

12.   Are there any examples of laughter through tears in THE ACCIDENTAL PRINCESS? Does this novel achieve a good balance between laughter and tears? If so, how?

13.   How does this novel create a sense of place? How might the story have been different if it were set

somewhere other than the Deep South?

14. The physical contrast between C.J. and Sandi Wentworth is dramatic. How does this contrast reflect the theme?

SPECIAL EDITION™

Continues the captivating series
from *USA TODAY* bestselling author

SUSAN MALLERY

**These heart-stoppin' hunks are rugged,
ready and able to steal your heart!**

Don't miss the next irresistible books in the series...

COMPLETELY SMITTEN
On sale February 2003
(SE #1520)

ONE IN A MILLION
On sale June 2003
(SE #1543)

Available at your favorite retail outlet.